THE HAUNTING OF CROW HOUSE

A.W. JAMES

This book is dedicated to the investigators of worlds unseen.

PROLOGUE

August 1st, 1892

Mary Cain fled through the moonlit woods, certain that her lungs would burst if she went any farther. But she dared not stop. The creature was right behind her.

She could hear it crashing through the undergrowth, a low growl escaping its throat, and she knew that if it caught her, it would drag her to the deepest pit of Hell, the very place from which it had surely been summoned.

She also knew that she could run no longer. She had barely eaten for the past four weeks, surviving on only the thin gruel and holy water her husband had given her while keeping her shackled to the bed. Her wrists were rubbed raw and bleeding from the cruel iron manacles she had worn during her month of imprisonment and she was sure that even if she managed to put a considerable distance between herself and her pursuer, the creature could simply follow the trail of blood she was leaving on the leaves and branches behind her.

And not only her wrists were bleeding; the front of her white nightgown was stained deep red from the knife wound that traversed her stomach. The wound stung like a thousand bee stings but she was sure the knife had not penetrated deeply enough to cause more than a superficial cut. That was due to her reflexes. She had instinctively sprung back when the blade had slashed at her. If not for that quick movement of avoidance, she was sure the cruel knife would have cut into her stomach and bowels.

Hot tears streaked down her cheeks, joining the ones that had dried there over the past weeks. She had endured so much but tonight her suffering would end, she was sure of that. Even if she could escape the foul demon that followed her, her old life was gone forever. She could never return to it, not after what she had discovered tonight. Better to let the demon take her.

But she feared for her soul. If the beast had truly come from Hell, then to succumb to it would mean being taken to the fiery pit to suffer eternal torment. It seemed she had no choice, as the legs she had barely used in the past month had wasted away and would not carry her much farther. And her lungs burned like the fiery pit which she was desperate to avoid.

Through the trees, she saw moonlight glinting off water. The lake. If she could get to it in time, she would not cheat death but she might yet save her soul. That shred of hope gave her a second wind, despite the searing pain in her lungs and screaming joints in her legs.

The beast continued at a steady pace behind her and let out a growl that almost sounded like a laugh. Mary wondered if the foul creature was mocking her. It seemed to be enjoying the chase. It was so close that she could smell the foul stench coming off its body yet it did not close the gap between her and it, even though she was sure it could grab her anytime it pleased.

I'll show you, she thought. *If I can get to the lake before you take me, I'll show you.*

Finally, she burst through the trees and onto a rocky promontory that jutted out over the lake. She knew this place; it was close to the house. She had stood here many times, in happier moments, looking out over the lake with her husband and daughter. The water was deep here, more than deep enough for her purposes.

Breathing hard, her raw wrists agonisingly painful, Mary paused for only a second before flinging herself from the rocks and into the water. During that second, she saw the glowing red eyes of the demon as it crashed out of the woods and onto the rocks. It did not seem concerned that it had lost its prey. On the contrary, Mary detected a vicious humour flicker across its inhuman features.

The lake was icy cold, despite the fact that it had been a hot July day today.

No, it's August, Mary reminded herself. *The first day of August. Lammas Day. I'm going to die on Lammas Day.*

She could not swim. During happier summers when she'd visited the lake, John and Elizabeth had frolicked in the water, splashing each other and swimming so far out it almost made Mary's nerves burst but she had always stayed on the shore, in the shade of the trees.

Now she was in the water and it was going to kill her. And in doing so, it would deny the demon her soul.

She knew that killing herself was a sin but surely God would see that she had only done so to avoid the fires of Hell and would take her to Heaven in His mercy.

But as she slipped beneath the surface of the cold water, she felt something grasp her ankle. She looked down to see a hand gripping her firmly. Then another hand appeared from the murky depths, and another. Until there were hundreds of fingers wrapping themselves around her feet, ankles, and thighs. The lake water was cold but the touch she felt on her legs was even colder, like a thousand fingers of ice grasping her legs.

And as the hands dragged her down into the watery darkness, Mary realised that the lake was not only deep, it was unfathomably so.

For it led all the way to Hell.

1

ARRIVAL

Present Day. July 25th

"Here we are," Mike Wilson announced, trying to summon up an enthusiasm he didn't feel. "Our new home." He parked the Kia Sportage in front of the low stone wall that surrounded the house, close to the black wrought iron gate.

"Do we really have to live here, Dad?" Jen said from the backseat. She'd looked up from her phone for the first time in an hour and was inspecting the house, a look of distaste curling her lips. "It looks old."

"It *is* old," he told her, "but that doesn't mean we can't make it into a nice home for ourselves." The truth was, Mike didn't like the look of the house either but beggars couldn't be choosers and right now, his financial status placed him firmly in beggar territory. He'd had a great job in London, heading the sales team of an advertising firm but the firm had gone bust thanks to the owners stretching the company's finances too thin and the whole thing had collapsed in a heartbeat. Mike found himself out of a job and looking for employment in a competitive industry that didn't seem to have room for him anymore.

Terri was making a little money selling her art but it wasn't enough to keep them afloat, especially with the exorbitant rent they'd been paying for their London flat. Their savings were being eaten up at an alarming rate just to pay for food and bills.

It was Mike's Uncle Rob who had come to their rescue. Mike hadn't seen his mother's brother in years but remembered him as a globetrotting relative who turned up to the occasional family get-together with stories of exciting adventures in various parts of the world. Mike had been surprised when Rob had called him out of the blue, saying that he had a job for Mike if he wanted it. There was a house in Derbyshire that Rob had bought a couple of years ago as an investment. The property was vacant and since Rob was currently travelling in the Philippines, he had no way of giving the place the attention it deserved.

He'd heard that Mike had fallen on hard times and offered him the house rent-free until he got back on his feet. All Mike had to do was tend to the neglected house and give it some much-needed care.

Left with no other options, Mike had convinced Terri and the kids and now, here they were. Uncle Rob's offer had felt a little too much like charity and that had left a bad taste in Mike's mouth but now that he saw the house, he realised he'd have his work cut out for him if he was going to get the place into shape.

Beyond the low stone wall, weeds and brambles had run rampant over the garden, strangling the life out of any flowers that may have once grown there. A flagstone path led from the gate to the front door but this too had been lost to the twisting tendrils of the weeds. The house itself was overgrown with vines and moss and some of the roof tiles were missing, pried loose by a length of creeping ivy which reached across the roof and down the walls and seemed to have claimed the house as its own.

Mike glanced at Terri in the passenger seat. She was staring at the house with a resigned look on her face and that hurt him more than any other expression her face might have shown. If she'd been horrified by the thought of the work ahead of them, that was one thing. If she were full of sorrow at the fact that their circumstances had brought them to this point, that was another. Mike could deal with those emotions by making light of the situation or assuring her that this wasn't for long and they'd be back on their feet soon. But this resignation, this dulling of the spark of life that usually lit her eyes, was something Mike had never seen before and it scared him.

"We'll be okay," he told her.

She looked at him briefly and then got out of the car without a word.

"I bet this place is haunted," Chris said from the backseat. "And I bet the ghost lives in your room, Jen."

"Shut up, dweeb," Jen said, rolling her eyes before looking down at her phone again.

"Are you getting a signal on that thing?" Mike asked, turning around in his seat to look at his daughter. The house was in the middle of nowhere, surrounded by bleak hills, thick woods, and not much else. The nearest village was a couple of miles away. He'd be surprised if there was a phone tower anywhere nearby.

"Barely," she said, showing him the screen.

The signal was just one bar. "This place really sucks."

"Who are you texting?" He'd seen that she was typing a message but hadn't had time to see whom she was talking to.

"Emma. I'm telling her this place sucks."

"Jesus, we've only just got here," Chris said. "Give the place a chance before you diss it to all your friends."

She looked at him and shot him a look of superiority. "You're just jealous because you don't have any friends."

"Shut up," Chris retorted before opening his door and getting out of the car. He slammed the door shut behind him and stormed off to the house.

"You should go easy on your brother," Mike said. "He's just as upset about this move as you are."

"Well he deserved it, telling me there's a ghost in my room."

Mike sighed. "There's no such thing as ghosts so just let it go."

"I know there's no such thing as ghosts, Dad, that isn't the point. The point is that Chris is always on my case. It's because he's a lonely geek and I have friends and a social life. Well, I had a social life before we moved to this Godforsaken place."

"Give it a chance, Jen. And as Chris's older sister, I expect you to look out for him; especially now we're going to be adjusting to a new place. Can you do that for me?"

She frowned at him. "He's fifteen, Dad, he's not a kid. He doesn't need anyone to look out for him, he should be able to do that for himself."

"Just humour your old man, okay?"

She let out a long sigh and rolled her eyes. "I'm not promising anything."

He knew that was the best response he'd get out of her right now. Everyone was tired from the four-hour drive they'd made to get here from London. It was a hot summer's day and the motorway had been a nightmare. It seemed that everyone in England was making the most of the weather, heading to their favourite summer destination, causing traffic jams everywhere. And there had been road works slowing the traffic even more. Miles and miles of road works.

"Right, let's take a look at our new home," Mike said, opening his door and getting hit by the summer heat. He'd never handled heat well and preferred cooler weather. Once the temperature rose above "pleasantly cool," he felt drained and irritable. That was all he needed at the moment when everyone's tempers were on a short, frayed fuse.

Terri and Chris were standing at the closed gate, staring at the abundance of weeds in the garden. Mike joined them and gestured to the gate. "Who wants to be first inside?"

"You've got the keys," Terri said flatly.

"All right, I'll lead the way." The gate scraped noisily on the flagstone path as Mike pushed it open. "Hinge is broken," he said, forcing it as far as he could before it jammed against the path. "That's job number one." He stepped through into the weed-infested garden and made his way to the front porch, kicking at the tendrils and vines that grabbed at his shoes.

The wooden porch felt surprisingly sturdy underfoot. Mike wondered if the property was in better shape than it had seemed at first. Maybe the only real work involved in getting the place ship shape was clearing the weeds out of the garden and the ivy and moss from the exterior walls. He stopped that thought before it went any further in his mind; he wouldn't be that lucky. There were probably leaking pipes and rotten floorboards inside.

He took the key ring that Uncle Rob had posted to him out of his pocket and found one that looked like it should fit the front door. He tried it in the lock but it didn't turn. "Maybe that one's for the back door," he mumbled to himself as he selected another key.

The second key turned in the lock and he heard a satisfying click as the latch opened. Terri and Chris had joined him on the porch and he fixed a smile on his face that was supposed to convey to them that he was optimistic about what lay beyond the door but probably just made him look silly. He pushed on the door and as it creaked open, he wrinkled his nose at the smell of musty air that rushed out of the house. At least it only smelled of dust and mildew. With the house being unoccupied out here in the wilderness, he wouldn't have been surprised to find dead animals inside.

Just because you can't smell them yet doesn't mean they aren't somewhere deeper in the house, he told himself. He stepped inside and found himself in a wide hallway with a black and white chessboard patterned tile floor. A wide flight of wooden stairs ascended to a landing before continuing up to the next floor. A naked light bulb hung from the high ceiling on a length of wire but Mike didn't need to turn it on because sunlight flooded in through a large semi-circular window above the landing.

"Wow," Chris said, walking into the hallway and turning around on his heels as he stared up at the high ceiling. "This place is huge. Can I look upstairs, Dad?"

"Of course," Mike said. "This is our home now."

Terri appeared at his side, arms folded, eyes appraising the hallway. "I have to admit, it looks better inside than it does from the garden."

The condition of the interior had surprised Mike too but he wasn't going to admit that. "Obviously the place is so well sealed that the elements and the weeds can't get in. That's good; it means the windows are all intact."

"We've only seen the hallway so far," she reminded him. "Let's have a look at the rest of the house before we declare this move a success."

"We'll make it work," he told her. "And we're only going to be here until I get a new job. Or your art takes off. You might be inspired by the countryside. Hey, maybe there's a spare room you can convert into a studio."

A flicker of a smile played over her lips. "Are you trying to bribe me into liking this place?"

He feigned an innocent expression. "Who me? Never."

She looked back out through the open front door, at the tree and the hills. "I suppose it might be nice to go for a walk every day and breathe fresh air for a change. Get back to nature."

"That's the spirit. Now, let's see what's through door number one." He went to the closest door and opened it. The room beyond was clean and tidy, with dark-stained wooden floorboards, a stone fireplace, and another bare light bulb hanging from the ceiling.

"Ugh, that wallpaper," Terri said, following him into the room.

Mike hadn't noticed the wallpaper but now that he looked at it, he didn't see anything wrong with it. It was a bit drab, he supposed but that was probably because the yellow colour had faded over the years. Maybe it was the fleur-de-lis motif Terri didn't like. "At least it's clean and dry," he said, running a hand over the smooth paper. "No rising damp."

Terri flicked a light switch by the door and the bulb sparked into life, giving off a sickly yellow glow. "It's a good thing this room has a big window," she said, "That bulb isn't doing its job. It's going to be dull in here at night time."

"I'll get some new bulbs," Mike offered. "There's bound to be a place nearby that sells them. The people in that village we passed have to get their groceries and essentials from somewhere." He decided to try and get her back into a more optimistic frame of mind. "Hey, this would make a great living room. There's plenty of space for the furniture and the TV. And we can build a fire at night. How's that for cosy?"

She glanced at the fireplace and then around the room. "I can see that it might have its charms."

Mike breathed out a sigh of relief. The state of the garden and the exterior of the house had made his heart sink but it was actually so nice inside that even Terri was coming around to the idea of living here. "Come on, let's check out the rest of the place," he suggested. "We get need to get dibs on the largest bedroom before Chris lays claim to it."

They went back into the hallway, where another door was now open, leading to a kitchen at the rear of the house. Jen was there, her back to Terri and Mike, staring out through a large window.

"See anything interesting, Jen?" Mike called.

She didn't respond.

"Well at least she's not staring at her phone for a change," Mike said to Terri as they walked toward the kitchen. When they entered the room, the first thing he noticed was that it was spacious and airy with windows running all the way along one wall. A marble-topped island sat in the centre of the room and a large oven was situated in an alcove that looked specially built for that purpose. The kitchen cupboards were fashioned of dark wood and the worktops were of the same marble as the island. Fluorescent strip lights ran along the ceiling.

Jen was standing by the sink, still staring out of the window. Mike could see an overgrown back garden out there, a low rear wall and gate, and beyond that, a small lake.

"Who needs a pool when you have a lake right outside the backdoor?" he said as he joined Jen at the sink.

She looked at him, blinking, her eyes distant. "Huh?"

"You okay, Jen?" Terri asked, concern in her voice.

Jen shook her head as if to clear it. "Yeah, I'm fine. I was just looking around and I saw the lake and...I don't know...I just tranced out or something."

Terri shot Mike a worried look.

"It's been a long journey," Mike said. "We're all tired. It's probably just your mind taking a break from all the stress." He put a hand on his daughter's shoulder. "This move hasn't been easy for any of us."

Jen shrugged. "It is what it is, Dad. I'm going to go and find a bedroom."

She went out into the hallway and Mike

shouted after her, "Not the biggest room; that one's for you mum and me."

From upstairs, Chris let out a long groan.

"Sounds like he'd already picked the big room," Terri said, smiling.

"That's my boy, always has big ambitions."

"But in this case, he's overreaching." she said.

"Uncle Rob didn't mention a lake," Mike said, looking out through the window. The high sun reflected off the shimmering water, making bright patterns of dancing light on the nearby trees. The movement was mesmerising, hypnotic. No wonder Jen had tranced out looking at it. Mike could see how staring at the flickering light might be restful after the long car journey they'd just endured. He could already feel his mind loosening, the tight muscles in his shoulders relaxing.

"Did Rob say why he bought this place? Did he live here at one time?" Terri asked.

"No," Mike said, pulling his gaze away from the lake. "He bought it on a whim, sight unseen. Rob does everything on a whim. He probably planned to flip the place and sell it at a profit but then his next adventure came along. He told me he's never even been here."

Terri raised her eyebrows. "He bought a

house he's never seen? He must have more money than sense."

"He said it was really cheap."

"I can't believe that. A big house in the middle of nowhere with a lake at the bottom of the garden? Depends on your idea of cheap, I suppose." She sighed and Mike sensed the resignation returning.

"Come on, let's go and find our bedroom and get the sleeping bags out of the car," he said.

Terri left the kitchen and Mike followed, resisting an urge to look out at the lake again. It seemed like a harmless action, to stare at the sunlight on the water for a while, but something deep in his subconscious, some part of him that was concerned with self-preservation, told him to resist the temptation.

2.

THE WARNING

It was early evening when Mike drove back along the road toward the village. Terri and Jen had opted not to come on this food run and were unpacking the boxes they'd brought to the house. Those boxes included some food items but Mike had suggested they get fish and chips from the village. He was sure he'd seen a chip shop when they'd driven through earlier, on their way to the house.

Chris was in the passenger seat, playing a game on his iPad. Mike could hear the whoosh of swords and shouts of pain coming from the iPad but he had no idea what the game was. "How are you doing, Chris?"

"I'm losing my castle to a bunch of dragons."

"I don't mean in the game, I mean with this move. You haven't said much about it. Your mum and Jen aren't happy that we came here and they tell me so at every opportunity. But you haven't said anything. I'd like to know your thoughts on the subject."

Chris shrugged. "It's fine. I don't really care one way or another."

"But you liked London."

"Yeah, sure."

Mike gestured at the trees lining the road and the rolling hills in the distance. "This is nothing like London."

"Dad, you need to get with the times. It doesn't matter where you are geographically anymore. Everyone is connected through the Internet. As long as I have a device in my hand, it doesn't matter if I'm in London or in a house in the country. It's all the same. Life is lived online these days."

"Well, your life is. Your eyes are always fixed on a screen."

"My point exactly. Everyone lives in a virtual world now. Everything we need is there."

Mike frowned at that. He knew his son spent a lot of time on a computer and he'd worried that Chris might be eschewing the real world but he hadn't realised it was this bad. "Not everything, Chris. Maybe you should take a look around you every once in a while, at things that are real. This is a beautiful part of the country. Some fresh air would do you good, instead of spending all your time on those games and chat rooms."

Chris raised an eyebrow. "Dad, you know that games and chat rooms are my life, right? I mean, this is going to be my job someday. This is how I'm going to earn a living."

"Yes, of course I know that but that doesn't mean you should ignore everything else."

"Maybe you should be more forward-thinking."

"What's that supposed to mean?"

Chris returned his attention to the iPad. "Nothing."

"No, come on, I want to hear what you have to say. You think I'm old-fashioned or something?"

"I didn't say that."

"No, but you implied it." Mike could see a sign ahead, half-obscured by the long grass at the side of the road. As he drove closer, he saw that it said *Shawby*.

"All I mean is that if you had a job working in IT, or if you had a knowledge of coding, then you wouldn't have...never mind, it doesn't matter."

Mike didn't push his son to finish the sentence. He knew what Chris was going to say: that if Mike had knowledge of computers, he wouldn't have lost his job. And by extension, they would still be in London, living their old life.

He didn't say anything else as they drove into the village, which consisted of a single main street lined with shops and a couple of side roads that led toward clusters of houses. Mike wondered if there'd be a chip shop here after all. There was a pub, of course, called The Shawby Arms and a corner shop that probably served the villagers' needs when they didn't want to drive all the way to Matlock, which was the closest town and which Mike knew had a supermarket. He scanned the other businesses as they drove by. An antique shop, a bookshop, a Chinese takeaway, and a charity shop.

"There's the chippy, Dad." Chris had lifted his head from the iPad long enough to have a look around and was pointing ahead of them. A lit sign showed an image of a cartoon fish carrying a bag of chips with the words *Shawby Fish Bar* beneath its tail.

Mike found a place to park among the half-dozen cars that were parked outside the establishment. When he looked through the windscreen into the brightly lit chip shop, he realised this was the most popular place in the village. A queue of people stood at the counter and others were sitting at plastic tables and chairs that had been set up inside, eating their meals. They got out of the car and entered the shop. Inside, the smell of oil in the fryers and battered fish behind the glass made Mike's stomach rumble in anticipation. But the heat was stifling. He had no idea how the two girls serving at the counter or the elderly man frying the chips could stand it.

By the time it was finally their turn to order, Mike wasn't sure what he was looking forward to more: getting their food or escaping the heat of the shop and getting outside where it was cooler.

"What can I get you, love?" the girl behind the counter asked him. He realised she really was just a girl, probably Chris's age. The other woman serving looked like an older version of her and was probably her mother. He gave her his order, which he'd written on a piece of scrap paper before leaving the house, and she busied herself fetching the food and putting it into cardboard boxes.

"All right, mate?" The elderly man, who was probably the owner, gave Mike a friendly nod as he lowered a fresh basket of chipped potatoes into the fryer.

"Hi," Mike said.

"I haven't seen your face before so I'm

guessing you're passing through? Or on holiday?"

Mike guessed that in a village like this, the chip shop owner probably knew all of his customers by sight, if not by name. "No, we've just moved here," he said. "So you'll be seeing a lot more of us from now on. I'm Mike and this is my son, Chris."

"I'm Stelios." He frowned, as if trying to remember something. "So, you've moved into the old Roberts' place on Ashtree Avenue, right?"

"No," Mike said, shaking his head. "We're not actually in the village. We're a few miles away."

Stelios grinned. "Well, I hope the chips are worth the drive."

"I'm sure they will be."

The girl finished packing their order into a paper bag and took Mike's money. After he got his change, Mike handed the bag to Chris. "Here, make yourself useful."

Chris raised his eyebrows and looked like he might protest but cast a quick glance at the girl behind the counter and said, "Sure, Dad."

When he opened the door onto the street, Mike felt a welcome breeze of cool air. He stepped onto the pavement and breathed deeply. "I thought I was going to suffocate in there," he told Chris.

As they reached the car, a voice from behind them said, "Excuse me.

Mike turned to face a man who appeared to be in his seventies. He sported a thick salt-and-pepper moustache and wore a flat cap. He was dressed in a tattered dark blue jumper and black trousers that were tucked into a pair of scuffed army boots.

"I heard you telling Stelios that you've moved into the area," the man said. "Excuse me for asking but it wouldn't be Crow House you've moved into, would it? Only I noticed that the house's lights were on earlier, for the first time in years."

"Crow House?" Mike frowned. Uncle Rob never mentioned that the house had a name. "No, I don't think so." He turned back to the car and opened his door.

"The house by the lake," the man said, grabbing Mike's arm.

Mike shook off the weak grip. Who did this man think he was, grabbing people in the street? And what business was it of his where they lived? He wasn't going to tell this stranger anything. "Get in the car, Chris."

While Chris climbed into the Sportage,

Mike turned on the old man. "Look, I don't who you are but you need to mind your own business. It's no concern of yours where my family lives. Now I suggest you leave us alone, go back into the chip shop, and order your food.

The man glanced at the Shawby Fish Bar, and then returned his attention to Mike. "I don't need to order. I have the same thing every week. Stelios will have it ready for me."

"Then I suggest you go and get it." Mike got into the car and shut his door.

"I only came to warn you," the man said, his voice muffled by the closed door. "About the house. About the lake."

"Who's that man, Dad?" Chris asked, watching the old man through the car window.

"No idea. Let's get home before the chips get cold." He started the engine and pulled onto the road before performing a U-turn that took them in the direction of their house. *Crow House*, Mike mused. *Is our new home actually called that or is that old man just crazy? Maybe he's talking about some other house.*

He looked over at his son. Chris was staring at the road ahead, the paper bag of food on his lap.

"You okay, Chris?"

Chris nodded. "Yeah, it's just...do you have a bad feeling about the house?"

Mike let out a long sigh. Chris hadn't mentioned any misgivings before about the house but now that a crazy local had shouted something about a warning, he was getting worried. "You know that guy was just talking nonsense, right? He's probably had his eye on the house for years and Uncle Rob outbid him or something. Don't worry about it, Chris."

Chris shrugged but remained silent.

"Hey, are you talking to me?"

"It isn't just what that guy said. When I went upstairs to choose my bedroom, I felt like I wasn't alone up there. Like someone was watching me. I kept looking over my shoulder, expecting to see someone standing there. And then, when I chose a room at the back of the house, I looked out of the window and I was sure I saw someone in the woods by the lake, watching the house."

"Why didn't you say something to your mum or me?"

"Because when I looked closer, it was just a shadow under the trees."

Mike recalled the bedroom Chris had chosen for himself after being turfed out of the master bedroom. "But your room isn't at the back of the house. It overlooks the front garden."

Chris nodded. "Exactly. I switched after I

thought I saw someone in the trees. And the lake freaks me out too."

"You have an overactive imagination, that's all."

"Whatever." He turned on his iPad and began playing the game again.

Mike spent the rest of the journey wondering if they were going to have any trouble from the old man. If their house was indeed the Crow House he'd referred to, that meant he knew where they lived. Hell, he might have been the person Chris saw from the upstairs window. They were going to have to be extra vigilant because if the old man had been crossed by Uncle Rob in some way, as Mike supposed, then who knew what he might do to take revenge?

But Mike didn't want to have to tell Terri that they might have a problem with this man. It was going to be one more thing for her to get angry about. Or be resigned about, which was even worse. One more thing for her to add to the list of *Reasons Mike Shouldn't Have Brought us Here*.

As he turned off the main road and onto the narrower road that led through the woods to the house, he decided to keep the strange encounter to himself.

3

THE CELLAR

As the house came into view, he felt a sudden sense of dread and understood what Chris had meant when he'd said the place was creepy. The house stood alone among the trees. Who knew what in those woods? Or maybe there was something hiding in the lake, ready to rise from the cold depths and crawl across the back garden toward the house.

You've been watching too many horror movies. The reason the house gives you a sinking feeling is because it's a reminder that you failed your family.

Trying to push that thought aside, Mike parked the Sportage in the same spot he'd chosen earlier and killed the engine. "Chips still warm?" he asked Chris, trying to inject a lightness he didn't feel into his voice.

"Yeah," Chris said, switching his iPad of and

opening the car door before trudging across the weed-strewn garden. Unlike Mike, Chris was making no attempt to hide his sullenness.

Mike sighed and got out of the car. When he reached the gate, which Chris had left open, he stepped through and closed it behind him, pausing to scan the trees that crowded around the house. Could someone be standing among the shadows, watching him right now?

He shook off the feeling of fear that had begun to creep up the back of his neck like an icy spider and turned from the gate, and the trees beyond, to face the house. He didn't feel welcome here but told himself that was because he was still missing London. Give it time and this place would feel like home.

He followed Chris into the house and found Terri in the kitchen. She had all the cupboards open and was attacking them with a duster. Mike could see that she'd also dusted the worktops and the marble island in the centre of the room.

"Where's Jen?" he asked.

She gestured to the open back door. "She went outside to look for firewood. She got the idea that we should light a fire in the fireplace and sit around it while we eat dinner." She mock-shivered. "That's actually not a bad idea. It's getting cold in here."

She was right; with the encroaching night, the temperature in the house had plummeted. There were heating vents in the floors, decorated with filigree metal grilles but when Mike held his hand over one, it was dead cold. "There must be a boiler somewhere," he said.

Terri pointed at a closed door. "That leads to a basement or cellar, so it's probably down there."

Mike opened the door. A narrow flight of wooden steps led down into darkness. "You been down there?" he asked Terri.

She shook her head. "No, it smells damp. I wouldn't trust those stairs if I were you."

He found a light switch on the wall inside the door and flicked it. Nothing. If there were lights down there, they weren't working. "Chris, can you go and get the torch from the car?"

Chris nodded and left the room.

"Mike, are you sure it's safe to go down there?" Terri asked, concerned.

"We're going to need to turn the boiler on at some point. Or we won't have any hot water."

"I know, but..." she cast a worried glance at the stairs that descended into darkness. "I don't want you going down there."

"It's just the cellar, Terri. Don't tell me this house gives you the creeps as well. Chris was just telling me he has a bad feeling about the place."

"Well, I was only worried about those old steps giving way beneath you but now that you mention it, yes, I do feel uncomfortable here." She looked around and hugged herself. Mike wasn't sure if the action was instinctual, or made purposefully to underscore her next sentence. "There's a bad atmosphere in this house."

He suddenly knew it had been a good idea to not tell her about the old guy in the village and his 'warning' about the house and lake.

Chris returned with the torch. It was small and metal-bodied and had a powerful beam. Mike clicked it on and shone it down the stairs. He could see a dirt floor down there in the circle of light. Beyond that, nothing but darkness. "The steps look solid enough," he told Terri before putting one foot carefully down onto the first one. It creaked beneath his weight but he was sure it was solid enough to hold him. He placed his other foot on the step. "No problem," he said, not sure if he was telling this to Terri or just reassuring himself. He kept the light trained on the section of floor at the foot of the steps.

"Do you want me to come with you, Dad?" Chris asked.

"No, Chris."

"Good, because there's no way I'm going down there."

Mike sighed. "You'll be thanking me later when we have a nice warm house." He stepped down onto the next step gingerly. It creaked loudly and he thought he heard something else along with the creak, something in the darkness below. A scuttling sound.

He took a deep breath and tried to relax. His heart was hammering in his chest. It's probably just rats, he told himself. He'd have to arrange for an exterminator to come and deal with them.

"Why have you stopped?" Chris asked from the doorway. "Are you scared?"

"Just making sure these steps are safe." But he felt frozen to the spot. That noise had unnerved him. He listened intently, straining to hear it again, but the only sound that reached his ears was the rhythmic drip drip drip of the kitchen tap. The drops of water hitting the stainless steel sink sounded like they were marking off time.

This is ridiculous, Mike told himself. There's no reason to be afraid. There's nothing down there in the dark except maybe a couple of rats. Taking a deep breath, he descended the remaining steps quickly until he was standing on the cellar's dirt floor. It was cool down here and it smelled musty. The air felt like a damp whisper as it passed over Mike's face. He shone the torch beam around.

The cellar was a square vault fashioned of bricks that had been sunk into the house's foundations. Mike saw some wooden shelves that seemed empty, gardening tools hanging from hooks that had been screwed into the walls, and a piece of furniture that might have been a desk. He let the light skip over these things as he searched for the boiler. Finally, he saw a pipe leading up into the house and below that, a large cast iron furnace. He sighed. He'd hoped to find a modern combi-boiler down here, something that would start working with the click of a switch. This furnace would have to be fed regularly with wood or coal and that meant regular trips down here.

Casting the light around in the hope of finding a pile of firewood next to the furnace, he discovered a single light bulb hanging from the ceiling. Following the wiring with the torch's beam, he found a switch on the wall at the bottom of the steps. He tried it and the bulb stuttered into life, casting a dull yellowish light over the cellar.

He turned it off and went back up the steps, leaving the torch on the top step, just inside the door in case he needed it again. In the kitchen, Terri and Chris were waiting with concerned looks on their faces. "Nothing to worry about," he told them, touched that were so concerned about him. "There's an old furnace down there so we're going to need that firewood Jen's collecting to feed it. We can get some more for the fireplace later. It's not like there's a shortage of wood around here." He glanced at the kitchen window. "I thought she'd be back by now."

"I'm surprised the smell of fish and chips hasn't brought her back," Terri said.

"I'll find her." Mike went out through the back door and into the overgrown garden. After making his way past the tangle of weeds that seemed determined to trip him over, he pushed through the gate and stood at the edge of the lake. Unlike earlier, when the sun had been reflecting off it, now the water looked dark and mysterious. He wondered how deep it was and picked up a small stone, which he tossed into the water a few feet from where he was standing. It hit the water with a loud splash and sank into the murky depths.

The realisation that he was standing so close to deep, dark water chilled him. He couldn't swim and had a fear of being deep enough that he couldn't touch the bottom with his feet. He sometimes had nightmares about drowning. On the rare occasions that he'd been to a swimming pool--when the kids were younger, mostly--he'd stayed in the shallow end. He'd thought it important that Jen and Chris learned how to swim and didn't want them to have the same horrendous experience he'd had.

When he was seven-years-old, his parents had taken him to the local pool and his dad had thrown him into the deep end, thinking Mike would swim instinctively. Instead, he'd sunk to the bottom, struggling to reach the surface but unable to fight against the weight of the water, which seemed to be dragging him down deeper despite Mike's frantic kicking and panicked arm flailing.

Finally, a lifeguard had jumped in and saved him. After pulling him to the surface and helping him clamber out of the pool, the lifeguard had thrown a few choice words at Mike's dad. That had been the end of Mike's swimming lessons and the beginning of the recurring nightmares about deep water that had plagued him all his life.

He walked toward the woods and called out Jen's name. When she didn't answer, he fought back a sliver of fear and told himself she probably had her headphones on. Fishing his phone out of his pocket, he called her number.

She answered after five rings, by which time, the sliver of fear was growing into full-blown panic.

"Dad?" She sounded like she'd been asleep.

"Jen, are you okay?"

She hesitated and then said, "Yes." She didn't sound very certain of that answer.

"Where are you?"

"By the lake. I came to..." she paused as if trying to remind herself of something. "Get firewood. I came to get firewood."

Mike scanned the edge of the lake. He couldn't see Jen but part of the lake disappeared behind a rocky promontory maybe a quarter of a mile from where he stood. Had Jen wandered that far from the house? There was plenty of firewood right by the gate so why would she wander away? "How far are you from the house?" he asked her.

"Umm, I don't know. Geez, Dad, don't have a heart attack. I'm on my way back, okay?"

He heard a scuffling sound on the line, presumably Jen getting to her feet, and then the call ended. He wanted to ask her why she was sitting by the lake when she was supposed to be collecting firewood but knew that in her present mood, she'd probably bite his head off. So while he waited for her to return, he busied himself collecting wood. By the time Jen appeared through the trees, he had scavenged an armful of branches and small logs. Jen wasn't carrying anything.

"Here," he said, passing her the bundle in his arms. "Take these to the house. I'll get some more. There's a furnace in the cellar so we're going to need plenty of this stuff."

She took the proffered wood and, without a word, trudged back to the house. Mike gathered more logs, concentrating on larger ones that would burn longer. He was going to have to build a woodpile in the cellar if they were going to have reliable heating and hot water.

When he got back to the kitchen, he dumped the wood next to the cellar door, where Jen had left her pile. He could sort the furnace out later; right now, it was time to eat.

"Let's get that food out, " he said. "I'm starving."

He helped Terri and Chris unwrap the fish and chips, his mouth watering as the smell of battered cod and salt-and-vinegar-covered chips reached his nose.

But for some reason, he lost his appetite slightly when he looked over and saw Jen standing at the kitchen window, staring out at the dark lake.

4

THE FACE

July 26th

Mike woke up the next morning with a stiff neck and a dull ache that had settled in his shoulder. He and Terri had slept on an airbed and he was sure his half of it had deflated during the night and that he'd ended up sleeping on the floorboards. Getting to his feet, he rubbed his eyes and squinted against the bright sunlight that streamed in through the window. His phone told him it was almost ten and that surprised him; he was usually an early-riser.

Wearily, he put on the same jeans and Pink Floyd T-shirt he'd worn yesterday. He hadn't bothered bringing any other clothes with him so the movers had better get here soon or he'd start to smell ripe.

The bathroom was at the end of the upstairs hallway and he trudged toward it as the last vestige of a dream danced in his head, just out of reach of his memory. Had he been dreaming of the lake? He was sure he had. He'd dreamed that he was standing on the shore and someone else was there with him, standing behind him as he stared into the cold depths. Even though the memory of the dream was elusive, there was something about it that scared him. He was almost afraid to remember it in case he remembered too much.

"Get a grip, Mike," he told himself as he entered the bathroom.

It looked like the room's decor hadn't been changed since the house had been built. The claw foot tub, substantial porcelain sink, and brass taps might well be the original fixtures from the house's Victorian past but Mike knew that a lot of modern bathroom fixtures were styled to look old and that might be what he was looking at now. The more he inspected the bathroom, though, the more he doubted that this room had been modernised. Everything looked genuine to him, including the oval-shaped mirror that hung over the sink, its silver frame fashioned into the shape of twisting vines. Mike ran his fingers over the smooth metal, tracing the upraised, twisting shapes. Someone had crafted this mirror with lot of care and a high degree of skill.

He turned on the tap and splashed cold water over his face, hoping it would wash away the final remnants of the dream. But when he lifted his face and looked into the mirror, what he saw there made him cry out in surprise.

He whirled around. There was no one behind him, yet he'd seen someone in the mirror, a dark-haired man standing there, staring at him.

From downstairs, Terri called, "Mike, are you okay?"

"I'm fine," he said, trying to keep his voice calm. His heart was hammering in his chest and he found breathing difficult. Leaning on the sink, he forced himself to take deep breaths and calm down. Whatever he'd seen, it must have just been a trick of the light or even a hallucination. Maybe his mind was still tired after yesterday's monotonous drive and was playing tricks on him.

But the man's face had seemed so real. Mike had clearly seen his reddish brown hair and close-cropped beard. The man's eyes had stared right into his via the reflection in the mirror.

They'd looked aggressive but also tinged with some sort of sadness.

Could he really have imagined it?

He dried his face and went downstairs to the kitchen, where Chris was leaning on the marble island, finishing a bowl of cereal. Terri stood at the back door, arms folded, a mug of steaming coffee in one hand as she looked out over the back garden.

"Mum's in a mood," Chris mumbled.

Mike nodded and went over to the coffee machine. He remembered arguing with Terri that the machine could go into one of the packing boxes and be transported by the movers but she'd insisted they bring it with them in the car, along with the sleeping bags, breakfast cereal, and long-life milk. Mike was glad she'd won that argument now; he needed the caffeine to kick-start his brain. As he poured a mugful of strong coffee from the pot, he closed his eyes and inhaled its rich aroma, as if the smell alone would clear his head of...

...of what?

...of ghosts?

He frowned at that thought. He was being ridiculous. The house wasn't haunted and he hadn't seen a ghost in the bathroom. He sipped the coffee quickly; ignoring the fact that it was so hot it was burning his tongue.

Chris sauntered over to the sink and dropped his bowl into it.

"Wash that up," Terri said, without taking her eyes off the garden. "The dishwasher won't be here until later and I don't want a dirty bowl hanging around when the movers get here."

"See," Chris said quietly to Mike as he turned the tap on and began to rinse the bowl. "I told you she was in a mood." After giving the bowl a cursory wash, he placed it on the worktop and threw the spoon into it. "That's the best I can do without any hot water."

Mike looked over at the wood by the cellar door. He needed to get the furnace going and it was going to take more wood than the couple of handfuls he'd brought in last night. "You just volunteered to collect the firewood today," he told Chris.

Chris groaned. "I wasn't complaining, Dad. I was just making an observation."

"I know. You're right, we need hot water. And to get hot water, we need to get the furnace going. And to get the furnace going, we need..." He paused, waiting for Chris to finish the sentence.

"Wood," Chris sighed.

"That's right." He gestured at the woods beyond the window. "And where do we find wood?"

"In the woods."

Mike detected something in Chris's voice that might have been fear. His son was no outdoorsman and had spent most of his life in the city but he'd been camping with Scouts when he was younger so there was no reason for him to be scared of nature. "You okay, Chris?"

Chris shrugged. "I'm fine."

"You can tell me anything, right?"

"Yeah, I know."

"So tell me what's wrong."

Looking out of the window, Chris said, "I told you yesterday, I think the woods are creepy."

"Spoken like a true city boy. You've seen too many horror movies, that's all."

Chris shook his head. "No, it isn't that. Maybe that man in the village knows something. He said he was going to warn us about the house and the lake."

"But he didn't say anything about the woods," Mike said, deciding to make light of the situation. "So you'll be just fine."

"Fine," Chris sighed. He left the kitchen, looking downcast.

"What's wrong with Chris?" Terri asked, coming inside to wash her mug.

"He's not too keen on going out to

the woods."

She looked out at the trees as she rinsed the mug. "I can't say I blame him. They're creepy."

"That's exactly what he said. I told him he's watched too many horror movies."

"He's not the only one. Every time I look at those trees, I'm reminded of *Friday the 13th*."

"I'm pretty sure that isn't Crystal Lake, Terri, and Jason isn't lurking around out there waiting for his next victim."

"Probably not." She shivered slightly. "But what is?"

"Nothing," he told her. "You and Chris are just spooked because you're used to living in a busy city. You probably feel isolated out here in the sticks. You'll get used to it."

"Well it's not affecting you or Jen. She went out for a walk early this morning. I've never know her to get up at the crack of dawn before, never mind going out without spending an hour or two getting ready. She didn't even take her phone with her."

"She's in the woods?"

Terri nodded.

"How long has she been out there?" He remembered calling Jen yesterday and how confused she'd sounded on the phone. Like she was lost.

"About an hour. And all that time, I've been

fighting the urge to run out there and find her and bring her back to the house where I can protect her."

She put her mug next to Chris's bowl on the worktop. "And I know you're going to say, 'protect her from what?' and the truth is: I don't know, Mike. All I know is that I'm scared for her and I don't want her going into those woods." She threw up her hands. "But she's old enough to make her own decisions. I don't have a say in what she does or doesn't do anymore."

"I'll go and check on her," Mike offered. "I'll help Chris get the firewood and while we're out there, I'll find out where Jen is."

"Okay," she said, nodding. "I know I'm being irrational but I can't help it."

"You're not being irrational," he told her, thinking of the face in the mirror. Had Terri seen something similar and was that why she was freaking out? "Have you seen something?" he asked. "Something that spooked you?"

She frowned, confused. "No, what do you mean?"

"Nothing," he said. No need to spook her further by telling her about the bathroom incident.

Chris reappeared from the hallway and said, "I might as well get this over with. I may be back later...or I may not." He put his hands on his hips and sighed dramatically, as if he were about to walk to the gallows.

"I'm coming with you," Mike said.

Chris's face brightened. "Really?"

Mike nodded. "And we'll see if we can get Jen to give us a hand as well."

"Okay, cool."

Because the house was in the countryside, Mike had brought a pair of old hiking boots with him in the car. They were siting in the hallway now, by the front door. He went to fetch them and returned to the kitchen to lace them up. Then he and Chris went out through the back door and fought their way past the weeds to the lake's edge.

The day was already warm and the water sparkled with sunlight. Mike watched the shimmering patterns of light until he realised dimly that Chris was talking to him.

"Huh?" He tore his eyes away from the lake. His head felt thick, as if it were filled with cotton wool. "What did you say?"

"I said there's plenty of branches here by the house. We don't need to go into the woods."

Mike cast a quick look at the area. Chris was right; there were dozens of branches lying around that would fuel the furnace just as well as anything they'd find in the woods.

But Mike needed to find Jen. He'd told Terri

he'd check on her. "No, come on, we're going to find your sister."

"Dad, I agreed to get firewood, not look for Jen."

Mike sighed. Chris had found a way to do what he was asked and also avoid going into the woods. Mike couldn't really argue against his son collecting firewood here because the fact that it was closer to the house meant there was less distance to carry it inside and that meant more could be collected in a shorter space of time.

"Fine," he told Chris. "You start collecting the wood and I'll find Jen."

Chris let out a long, low breath like a man who'd just been granted a stay of execution.

"Chris, we're going to have to talk about your fear of the woods. It isn't healthy. You're going to have to face it and get over it."

"I'll do that," Chris said, "just not right now." He quickly began picking up sticks and branches, probably scared that Mike would change his mind and make him go into the woods after all.

Mike considered doing just that; Chris's aversion to the woods wasn't rational. And neither was Terri's. But he could fight that battle later. For now, he needed to find Jen.

He left Chris to it and walked along the

lake's edge to the trees. Wondering if she should call out for Jen but then deciding not to, he entered the woods. Despite the warmth of the day, the shadows beneath the overhanging branches were cool. The sweet scent of wildflowers hung in the air, tinged with the smell of rotting wood and fungus. Mike searched the area for a path that Jen might have followed but the wild undergrowth had grown over any trails that might have once been here so he skirted the lake, keeping it in view at all times so he wouldn't get lost.

As time wore on, the impenetrable gloom began to feel oppressive and Mike felt as if the trees were crowding closer, trying to crush him. He spied the rocky promontory that jutted out into the lake and decided to walk over to it, if only to get out from beneath the thick canopy of foliage that blotted out the sky.

As he moved toward the sunlight, it suddenly seemed too far away and the need to reach it as soon as possible became imperative. He'd never suffered from claustrophobia before but here in the shadows beneath the towering trees, he could understand why some people feared enclosed spaces.

He tried to reason with himself. He was in the woods, not an elevator or a dark crawlspace. There was nothing to fear here.

But by the time he reached the rocks, the feeling of being stifled by the trees had grown into a very real terror and he was almost running for the edge of the woods. When he finally broke out from the shadows and stood on the sunlit rocks, he gasped for breath, his heart pounding.

He turned to look back the way he'd come, half-expecting to see the trees lunging forward toward him but all he saw was broken branches and trampled undergrowth where he'd made a panicked dash out of the gloom between the tall trees.

He felt embarrassed now he was on the rocks, the bright sunlight warming his face. At least no one had seen him running like a frightened child out of the woods. Chris would have had a field day.

He could see the house from where he stood. Chris was dutifully collecting firewood and had built a small pile of logs by the garden wall.

Mike turned his attention to the rocks where he was standing and discovered that the promontory was topped with a large flat rock, its surface worn smooth by the soles of many boots tramping over it. Derbyshire was popular with hikers and Mike assumed that the lake would be a local beauty spot. It was idyllic, after all, nestled away among the trees. Maybe people came here to swim.

If he needed further proof that others had visited this place, it was provided by sets of initials scratched into the rock. He walked farther out onto the promontory to take a closer look.

When he got closer, though, he realised that the carvings were symbols. He knelt down to inspect them, running his fingers over the indentations that had been scratched carefully into the rock.

The first one he touched, the one closest to him, was a pentagram. He knew it was an occult symbol but he'd seen enough pentagrams spray-painted on walls and under bridges in London to know that it was a popular symbol for graffiti artists. Probably just some local kids who thought they were Satanists or something.

The next symbol he came across, though, was more complex. It was a design he couldn't remember seeing before yet something about it gave him the chills, despite the brightness of the summer morning. There was a pentagram again but this time it was within a circle. And on top of the circle was a crescent moon, its twin points facing upwards so that the moon might also represent horns.

At the very edge of the rock slab, he found a third and final engraving. This time, it actually *was* initials, and Mike wondered if they'd been put there by some random hiker or by the same person who carved the occult symbols. He guessed the latter. Something about the way the letters were scratched into the rock suggested they had been put there by the same hand that had made the pentagram designs.

E. C.

The letters could stand for anything. They didn't even indicate whether the person who put them there was male or female. Mike ran a few names through his head. Evan, Evelyn, Ethan, Erica. And the C could be Carter, Campbell, Cooper, or even Chisholm.

He'd probably never know who the initials actually belonged to so he decided they'd been put there by a lone hiker named Evelyn Carter who'd discovered the lake by accident while walking in the woods and put her initials on the rock so that she would see them the next time she came here and be reminded of her previous visits. But she was never able to find the lake again and the only proofs that she'd ever been here at all were the letters of her name carved into the rock.

"Which I shall now refer to as Evelyn's Rock," Mike told himself, pleased with his story. He knew his attempt at levity was a reaction to the fear he'd felt in the woods and the nervousness he felt about the symbols that were scrawled into the rock but it still made him feel better.

He took a deep breath to psych himself up and prepared to go back into the woods. He still needed to find Jen. He was about to take the first step toward the trees when a voice reached him from across the lake.

It wasn't the spirit of the mysterious "E.C." or a water-borne ghost, or even a mermaid. It was just Chris, standing at the edge of the lake by the house, waving his arms to get Mike's attention.

"Dad! Over here!"

Mike waved back and shouted, "Hey, Chris. You're doing a good job there."

Chris pointed at the woodpile he'd created and then gave Mike a thumbs up.

"Your sister hasn't come back yet has she?" Mike asked hopefully.

Chris shook his head. "Maybe the ghost got her."

"Stop that, Chris. I told you it's—" He stopped when he noticed something in one of the bedroom windows. He put up a hand to shield eyes from the sun, certain that he couldn't be seeing what he thought he was seeing. But the more he looked at the window, the more certain he was that there was a face behind the glass, looking down at Chris.

A man's face with brown hair and a beard. The same face Mike had seen in the bathroom mirror.

He pointed at the window, jabbing his finger in the air so Chris would turn around and see the face. His son did turn around and look at the house but Mike realised that from this distance Chris couldn't know which particular window was being pointed out to him. Chris's head moved from left to right as he looked over the house. The face continued to stare down at him but Chris seemed oblivious.

"The window," Mike shouted. "The upstairs window."

Chris turned back to face him and shrugged.

Mike pointed again. "There, in the upstairs window."

Chris turned to the house again, his gaze roaming over the upstairs windows but not settling on the right one, the one with the man's face behind it. The brown eyes continued to glare down at the boy.

Was it just a trick of the sunlight on the windowpane or was Mike losing his mind? No, he refused to believe either of those things. He could see the man's face as clearly as he could see Chris's.

He fished his phone out of his jeans pocket and jabbed at the camera app. He aimed it at the house and checked the screen. The man's face was just as clear in the image on the screen as it was to the naked eye. Mike took a photo, then another, and then a third. After they'd been saved, he pulled them up and checked them. He wasn't going mad; the bearded face was present in all three photos.

"What is it, Dad?" Chris called across the water.

Mike was already clambering over the rocks and back into the woods, his previous fear of the trees replaced by a burning need to get back to his family. Someone was in the house. As he crashed through the undergrowth, he used the phone to call Terri.

She answered immediately, her voice panicked. For a moment, Mike wondered if she was aware of the stranger in the house with her but then realised she was probably worried because he'd gone into the woods to find Jen and now he was ringing her. She probably thought something was wrong. "Did you find her?"

"Get out of the house," he said, trying to

keep his voice steady as he ran. "There's someone in there. A man. Upstairs."

"What?" She sounded fearful now. Mike could hear movement on her end of the line and assumed she was leaving the house by the back door.

"Are you out?"

"Yes, I'm in the garden. Chris is here too."

"Stay there. Don't go back in the house."

"I'm calling the police."

"Fine, just stay outside. I'll be there in a—" He tripped over a hidden root and went sprawling into the undergrowth. He hit the ground hard, the air exploding out of his lungs as his chest slammed into more thick roots. His face hit the ground and he tasted soil.

Scrambling to his feet, he leaned against a big pine tree while he tried to regain his breath. Then he realised he'd dropped his phone. He spotted it lying a few feet away and quickly scooped it up, increasing his pace into a run again bit slower this time, more cautious. His ribs ached and there were stinging scratches and grazes on his arms. His movement was less a run and more a painful lurch forward.

He checked the phone. Terri had hung up. She was probably calling the police.

Navigating his way through the trees as fast as he could while also being careful of hidden dangers in the undergrowth, Mike reached the edge of the woods in five minutes. Terri and Chris were standing by the low rear wall, staring at the windows.

"There's no sign of anyone," Terri said as Mike approached. "Are you sure there's someone in there?"

"I saw someone," he told her. "At one of the upstairs windows. A man."

"What should we do?"

"Did you call the police?"

She nodded.

Mike considered his options. The police would take ages to get here and by then, the man would probably have gotten away. "I'm going inside," he said.

"Don't be stupid."

"I'll get a knife from the kitchen drawer."

"And he might have an axe. We need to wait here until the police arrive."

Mike knew she was right. Charging around the house with a knife wasn't going to help anyone and might get him killed. But he felt so angry at this invasion of their home that he couldn't just do nothing. "I'll go around to the front of the house so he can't get away."

"No, Mike, you're not playing the hero. There isn't anything he can steal anyway; the house is empty apart from a few sleeping bags.

Besides, you don't look like you're in any condition to fight a burglar. You're covered in dirt and your T-shirt is ripped. What happened?"

"I fell over." He hadn't realised his T-shirt had been ripped but when he inspected it, he found a tear on the right shoulder and another on the left sleeve. "Great. One of my favourite T-shirts too."

Terri raised an eyebrow. "You've virtually lived in that T-shirt every weekend for the past ten years. It's time to move on."

He was going to say something like, "Maybe you should be as philosophical about us moving here" but decided against it. This was hardly the time to get into another argument with Terri. And he couldn't exactly put a positive spin on the move when the new house had just been broken into.

"Listen," Chris said. "The police are here."

Mike listened. In the distance, a siren wailed. "I'll go out to the front of the house and meet them," he said, pushing thorough the rear gate before Terri could stop him. He had to make sure the man in the house couldn't get away. If he waited behind the house while the man ran out the front and escaped, Mike would never forgive himself.

"Mike, come back!" Terri shouted after him

but he ignored her and went into the house. He didn't stop to pick up a knife in the kitchen, afraid that if he did so, he might give the intruder time to escape. Instead, he ran to the front door and flung it open before going out into the front garden. Then he waited, his gaze fixed on the open door. If the intruder came down the stairs, Mike would see him.

The police siren was louder now and Mike risked a quick glance along the road. A dark green Range Rover was speeding toward the house, a single flashing light affixed to its roof. It looked like a plain-clothes police vehicle, not the patrol car Mike had expected.

It skidded to a stop by the gate and the siren went dead. The man who climbed out of the passenger side looked to be fit and in his late fifties. He was dressed in a cream-coloured shirt, black tie and trousers. His shirtsleeves were rolled up to the elbow, revealing tanned, muscular forearms. His salt and pepper hair was neatly combed, the moustache he sported neatly groomed. His eyes were hidden behind sunglasses.

A woman got out of the driver's side. She was much younger than her colleague. Mike guessed her to be in her late thirties. She also wore shades and was neatly presented but where the man's hair was greying and short, she had a long mane of straight black hair that reached below her shoulders. Her attire consisted of a dark blue skirt and white blouse.

The man reached Mike first, extending his hand in greeting and drawing Mike into a powerful handshake. "DCI Battle," he said. "And this is DS Lyons. We were told you have an intruder, sir."

Mike guessed that crime must be really low in this area for the force to send a Detective Chief Inspector and a Detective Sergeant to a simple burglary.

"We were in the area," Battle explained, as if reading Mike's mind, "So you get us instead of a couple of uniforms." He directed his attention to the house. "Wait here, sir, while we check the property." He and DS Lyons entered the house by the open front door.

"I think he's upstairs," Mike called after them.

"Don't worry, sir," Battle said, turning toward the stairs. "If he's still here, we'll find him."

Mike waited, expecting to hear a commotion inside the house when the two detectives found the intruder. But after a few minutes, Battle emerged from the house. "Can't see anything, sir. He must have fled. Although he seems to have taken all your furniture with him." He shot Mike a wry smile.

"We've only just moved in," Mike explained. "The movers will be here later today."

DS Lyons came outside to join them. "Was the front door open like this, sir, or was it closed?"

"It was closed. I opened it just now. I wanted to make sure he couldn't escape so I came out here. My wife and son are at the back gate." He had no idea how the intruder could have escaped. Unless he'd left by the front door while Mike was still in the woods. But would he have closed it behind him after fleeing? It seemed unlikely.

"No broken windows," Battle said.

"Mike, what's going on? Have they caught him?" Terri appeared at the front door with Chris by her side.

"Ah, Mrs Wilson, I presume," Battle said, striding over to her and shaking her hand. "You called us about a possible intruder. We checked the house but we couldn't find anyone, I'm afraid."

Mike noted that in Battle's mind, the intruder had now been downgraded to *possible* intruder.

"Could you give us a description of the man you saw?" Lyons asked.

"Well I didn't see him. It was my husband who saw him. I called you while he was coming back to the house."

Battle frowned. "I'm sorry, ma'am, but I'm confused. Coming back to the house?"

"I was in the woods at the time," Mike explained. "Well not in the woods exactly but standing on a rock that juts out into the lake."

"I think you're going to have to show me this rock, sir, so we can get a clear picture of what you mean."

"Of course, it's this way." Mike led them through the house and out into the back garden. "There," he said, pointing at the promontory. "That's where I was standing. I was looking at the house and I saw a face in the upstairs window."

Battle shielded his eyes against the sun and looked out over the lake. "That's quite a distance, sir."

Mike narrowed his eyes. Was the detective implying he was mistaken? That he couldn't see a face from that far away?

Battle pushed through the back gate and walked to the lake's edge before turning around and gazing at the upper windows. "Quite tricky to see details at a distance, sir. Are you sure it wasn't the sunlight on the windowpane? A shadow perhaps?"

"Very sure," Mike said, pulling his phone from his pocket. "I have photos." He found one of the pictures that showed the face at the window and held his phone out to Battle. "Look at this."

Battle came back in through the gate and took the phone from Mike. He inspected the picture closely and then handed the phone to Lyons. "See anything?"

She looked at the phone and shook her head. "I can see the windows but no face."

"What?" Mike snatched the phone from her hand. "It's right here, look." He zoomed in on the face in the window and pointed at it. "It's unmistakable."

She frowned at the picture and then shook her head again. "Sorry, sir, I don't see a face."

He held the picture up to Terri. "Tell me you see it. It's plain as day."

Terri took the phone from him and held it close to her face. "There's nothing there, Mike. It's just a window."

"Chris," Mike said, grabbing the phone and thrusting it at his son. "You can see the face, can't you?"

Chris examined the picture, squinting at it, and after a couple of seconds, pointed at a section of it. "Maybe this shadow here might look like a face if you were far away."

"I'm not misinterpreting shadows," Mike said, taking the phone from his son. The face in the photo was as clear to him as Chris's face was right now. There was no doubting what it was. Why couldn't anyone else see it?

"Mr Wilson," Battle offered, "Perhaps you had the sun in your eyes and you thought you saw someone at the window. And now, when you look at the picture, you're remembering what you think you saw, instead of seeing what's actually there. Or not there, in this case."

What Battle was suggesting was outlandish and Mike didn't believe a word of it. But what was the alternative? That he was losing his mind? "I'm sorry for wasting your time," he mumbled. He had no idea how he could see the face in the photo when nobody else could but he refused to believe he was going crazy. The face was there. He'd seen it when he was standing on Evelyn's Rock and he could see it now in the picture.

The fact that he'd seen the exact same face in the bathroom mirror this morning gave him pause. He'd been alone in the bathroom. There had been no one else there. So maybe this was a figment of his imagination as well.

"No problem at all," Battle said. "Better safe than sorry. Enjoy your new home. And I mean this in the nicest possible way but I hope we won't be seeing you again anytime soon."

Terri smiled at him. "I'll see you out." She led the two detectives back through the house and out into the front garden. Mike followed, feeling numb. His mind raced, trying to find a logical explanation for the events that had just occurred. But the only reasonable explanation he could come up with was that he was losing his mind.

What about unreasonable? he wondered desperately. The obvious unreasonable explanation was, of course, ghosts. This bearded man was haunting the house for some reason and only Mike could see him.

It sounded absurd. First of all, he didn't believe in ghosts. And secondly, why would he be the only person able to see one? He was hardly psychic or sensitive or whatever it was they called someone who was apparently attuned to the spirit world.

As he stepped out through the front door, a rumbling sound in the distance interrupted his thoughts.

"Here comes all that furniture the burglar would have stolen," Battle said.

The moving company's lorry ambled along the road toward the house, shaking as it drove over the potholes in the road.

"They're early," Terri said.

"Well at least you'll have more time to get yourselves sorted," Battle said, removing the light from the roof of the Range Rover. He hesitated before getting into the vehicle, as if making a decision. Then he came back to Mike and handed him a business card with his name and phone number printed on it. "Don't hesitate to call us again if you need us." He returned to the Range Rover, gave a little wave, and shut the car door.

Lyons offered Terri a smile before climbing in behind the wheel and starting the engine. Mike wondered if the smile was one of pity. After all, in the Detective Sergeant's eyes, Terri was living with a husband who was losing his marbles.

The Range Rover performed a U-turn and drove away, passing the oncoming lorry carefully before increasing speed and disappearing into the distance. The lorry came to a stop outside the gate, smelling of gasoline and hot metal. The engine died and the two young men inside jumped down from the cab.

Mike looked at the overgrown garden around him and said to Terri, "We should have cleared a path through the weeds. They'll have a hell of a job fighting through them while they're carrying our stuff."

He began kicking at the chaotic, twisting mass of vines and stalks, trying to form a clear route for the movers when something caught his eye. A piece of black wrought iron that matched the gate.

He reached into the tangle of weeds where it lay and ripped it from the grasping tendrils that had grown over it and claimed it as their own.

"What's that?" Terri asked him.

"It's a nameplate. It was probably attached to the gate at one time." He turned it over in his hands and read the two words formed by the curling black metal.

Crow House.

5

THE KEY

AN HOUR LATER, while Mike was standing at the front of the house, directing the movers, his phone buzzed in his pocket. He checked the screen. The number wasn't recognised by the phone; it was simply a string of digits. He was sure the area code was a local one, though.

"Hello?"

It was Jen's voice on the other end of the line. "Dad, can you come and pick me up?"

"Jen, where are you?"

"I'm in the village."

"What? What are you doing in the village?"

"I walked here, I guess."

"You guess?"

"I walked here," she said, her voice firmer. "I'm in a phone box outside an antiques shop on the main road. Are you going to pick me up or shall I walk back?"

"I'm on my way," he said.

"Who was that?" Terri asked, coming out of the house.

"Jen. She's in the village."

"What? What's she doing there?"

"She walked there apparently. I'm going to go and pick her up. Are you okay overseeing things here?"

"Yes, of course. Go."

He climbed into the Sportage and backed out past the moving company's lorry before spinning the wheel to turn the vehicle so that it was facing the right way. Then he pressed the accelerator pedal as much as he dared on the narrow road that led through the trees. He hadn't been overly concerned about Jen earlier but now, a spider of worry was beginning to nest in his mind.

Going for a morning walk in the woods was one thing but why had she wandered so far? He estimated the distance between the house and Shawby to be at least five miles. Jen didn't like walking that much. In London, she got the tube or taxis everywhere. She once complained that a walk along Oxford Street had "done her feet in." And now she'd hiked five miles through the woods?

He was still pondering the situation when he reached Shawby and spotted Jen standing by a phone box. She waved at him, although it seemed half-hearted, as if she didn't have the strength to raise her arm. When Mike pulled up next to her and she got into the passenger seat, he was surprised by how pale and tired she looked. But maybe that was to be expected after her long walk.

"You okay?" he asked.

"Yeah, fine." She looked and sounded sullen. While Mike jockeyed the Sportage around so it faced back the way he'd come, Jen simply stared out of her window.

"How was the walk?" he asked her when he finally got the car facing in the right direction.

She shrugged, saying nothing.

He sighed. It was going to be one of those days. Deciding to try one more time before letting her sink into a silence that would last for the entire journey, he said, ""Hey, we found out the house has a name. It's called—"

"Crow House. I know."

"But how can you know? We only just found out."

Jen shrugged again. "I'm sure someone told me."

"Have you been speaking to anyone in the village?"

"Only the girl behind the counter at the corner shop. I was thirsty so I got a Coke."

"Did *she* mention Crow House?"

"I don't think so." She furrowed her brow and seemed to be thinking. Then she said, "I'm not sure where I heard it."

"Chris didn't say anything to you about the guy we saw at the chip shop last night?"

"No, what guy?"

"It doesn't matter." He could only assume Chris had mentioned Crow House to Jen last night and now she couldn't recall where she'd heard the name.

They drove the rest of the way without saying a word to each other but Mike didn't think Jen had fallen into a sullen silence. Instead, he got the impression that she was mulling something over in her head. When he glanced over at her, she was watching the trees roll by her window with a thoughtful look on her face.

She's probably trying to figure out where she heard the name Crow House, he told himself.

He wanted to tell her that next time she went walking, she had to take her phone with her but that could wait; if he started laying down the law now, she'd probably rebel and either give up walking forever and spend her time moping around the house or she'd make a point of never taking her phone anywhere.

The latter scenario seemed unlikely, though. Jen was usually so attached to her phone that Mike had once asked her if it was permanently grafted to her hand.

When they got back to the house, the movers were closing up the back of the lorry and getting ready to leave. Mike parked far enough away that the lorry could turn around to head back up the road and gave the two men a quick wave as he joined Terri at the gate.

"That didn't take long," he said.

"We haven't really got much stuff. It seemed like a lot in our small flat but now it's in this house, I realise how little we actually own. The rooms still look empty."

"We'll get some more over time," he told her. "We'll soon fill up the place and make it seem like home."

She frowned at him. "Is that what you want, Mike? Because I thought the plan was to move back to the city. This..." she turned toward the house and threw up her hands. "This isn't us."

"It's a change, sure, but we'll get used to it."

"And what if I don't want to get used to it? What if I want to live in a city? Where there are other people and places to go and everything isn't so isolated?" She turned on Jen. "And you, young lady. Where the hell have you been? You told me you were going for a walk in the woods. I thought you'd be back after half an hour, not end up in a village miles away."

Jen just shrugged, ambled across the front garden and disappeared into the house.

"She probably just lost her way," Mike said. "There aren't any paths to follow."

"All the more reason for her not to go there," Terri said. "What if she actually gets lost and can't find her way back here or to the village? We don't want to have to call that detective again. First faces in windows and then our daughter missing in the woods. He'll think we're crazy."

"He already thinks I'm crazy," Mike said.

"No, he doesn't."

"Of course he does. You saw the way he looked at me. Like he was ready to commit me to the nearest mental hospital."

"Well you were acting strangely."

He decided not to defend his position. Doing so would only lead to an argument and there was no way he could convince Terri that he'd seen a man at the window, even with photographic evidence.

"I'll go and light the furnace," he said and

sauntered into the house, leaving Terri at the gate. There was once a time in their relationship when they'd have stuck up for each other, no matter what, but he supposed he couldn't expect her to say she saw a face in a picture when she saw nothing at all.

"Come on, Chris, we need to get that wood down to the cellar."

Chris looked up from the laptop and then over at the cellar door. His face took on a worried look.

"No, I don't want to hear it," Mike said, nipping whatever protest was about to come out of his son's mouth in the bud. "You can't be scared of the woods *and* the cellar. There's nothing down there except for some old gardening tools. Now give me a hand with the wood."

Chris followed him to the back door and across the back garden to the gate, a glum expression fixed to his face.

"Cheer up," Mike said. "As soon as we get this done, we'll have hot water. You get dibs on the first shower."

"We don't have a shower," Chris informed him, picking up an armful of wood from the pile he'd made earlier. "Just an old bathtub."

"Well you get dibs on the first bath, then."

Mike loaded his arms with as much wood as he could carry and together they trudged back across the garden and into the house.

When they got to the cellar door, Chris held back. "You first," he offered.

"Get the door for me. You aren't carrying as much as I am."

Chris opened the door and Mike stepped carefully down onto the first step, leaning back slightly in case the extra weight he was carrying overbalanced him and sent him tumbling into the darkness below.

When he got to the bottom, he managed to find the light switch and flick it. The dim bulb glowed weakly. Mike decided that when he went on a bulb run, he was going to get a powerful one for down here. Maybe a daylight bulb. The light from this old thing wasn't even illuminating the shadows in the corner of the room.

He went to the furnace and dropped his armful of wood in front of it like an offering. "Come on, Chris." He heard hesitant footfalls on the steps, and then Chris appeared in the dim light, his face hidden behind the logs he was carrying. "Just throw them down here," Mike told him.

Chris dumped the wood and looked around

the cellar, wrinkling his nose. "It stinks down here. Like something died in the walls."

"It's just old air and a bit of damp," Mike said. "Once the furnace heats up, everything will dry out down here."

"What's this?" Chris asked, going over to the piece of furniture in the corner, his fear seemingly overridden by curiosity.

"A desk, I think," Mike said, remembering seeing the piece of furniture in his torch beam yesterday.

"Weird desk," Chris said.

Mike went over to the shadowy corner to take a look. "It's a bureau. People used them for writing. This part here folds down." He went to pull down the fold-down writing table but it was locked. There was a large keyhole decorated by a brass surround but no key that Mike could see. "Maybe the key is in one of the drawers," he said and bent down to try the four drawers—two large and two small—beneath the writing part of the bureau. But they were also locked and each bore a keyhole identical to the one on the fold-down table.

"We could bust it open," Chris suggested.

"Why?" Mike asked. "I was only going to show you how it works."

"But there might be something inside it.

Something valuable. It looks old and old stuff is valuable, right?"

"Yeah, sometimes, but the bureau, along with anything inside it, belongs to my Uncle Rob. It's part of the house, so he owns it. We can't go breaking into it."

Chris shrugged. "Okay."

Mike wondered at Chris's cavalier attitude to stealing—or damaging—someone else's property. If *he'd* suggested something like that to his own father when he was young, he'd have had his ass kicked all the way up the cellar steps and out of the house.

"Chris, breaking stuff is not okay."

"Yeah, you said."

"Go upstairs and get me some of the packing paper from one of the boxes and some matches. We need to get this furnace going."

Chris sauntered away in silence.

Left alone in the cellar, Mike took another look at the bureau in the corner. There was no way he was going to break into it but he would like to find the key if it still existed. Whatever was inside the drawers—if there was anything inside them at all—might date back to the house's original occupants.

He wasn't exactly a history buff but he was curious about who had lived in Crow House.

There might even be something inside the bureau that would reveal the identity of the mysterious *E.C.* whose initials were inscribed in the rock by the lake.

He also had another thought that he tried to shake from his head. The contents of the bureau might tell him who the bearded man in the window was. He dismissed the thought as soon as it arose because if he thought the clue to the man's identity was in Crow House's past, then he was acknowledging that the face he'd seen was that of a ghost. And despite the weird events he'd experienced since coming to the house, he wasn't ready to fall down that particular rabbit hole just yet.

"Besides, the damn thing might be empty," he told himself. "Just a piece of junk sitting in the cellar of an old house."

So why was it locked?

And it was hardly junk; the bureau was finely crafted from a wood that Mike guessed to be high-quality mahogany. He didn't know anything about antiques but he recognised craftsmanship when he saw it.

On an impulse, he bent over and put his arms around one end of the bureau, hooking his fingers beneath it. When he straightened his legs to lift the piece of furniture, he discovered that it was damned heavy. Still, he continued his attempt to lift one side, reasoning that if there was anything inside, he'd hear it moving around in there, at least answering the question of whether or not the drawers were empty.

He put his back and legs into the task and managed to raise one end of the bureau off the floor. He was rewarded by the sound of something sliding inside one of the drawers and coming to a stop with a *thunk*.

That answered his question. There was something in there. He lowered the bureau gently back to the floor.

Chris reappeared, trailing a length of packing paper behind him. He handed Mike a box of matches and let the paper fall to the floor.

"Thanks," Mike said, opening the heavy iron door of the furnace and stuffing the paper inside.

"If you don't need me for anything else, I'm going to go back upstairs," Chris said. He sounded bored but Mike wondered if he was still frightened of the cellar and was faking the bored tone to hide his fear.

"Sure, go ahead." He added wood to the pile of paper in the furnace, struck a match and threw it in. The flame caught the paper and began to spread, licking at the smaller pieces of wood. While the fire established itself, Mike decided to inspect the various gardening tools hanging on the wall, hoping to find something heavy duty that would help him attack the weeds and vines that had taken over the garden.

The tools seemed old but at least they weren't Victorian. Along with a spade and a rake, there was a pair of shears and a trowel, as well as a leaf blower. But the thing that looked most enticing to Mike was an electric grass trimmer. He could imagine himself attacking the weeds with that in his hands. The other implement hanging there that would probably make short work of the weeds but might be too dangerous to use was a hand scythe. Mike had never used one and decided the trimmer would be the safest choice.

He checked on the fire, saw that it was burning nicely, and added some more wood before shutting the furnace door. He took the trimmer down from the wall and was about to leave the cellar when he heard something behind him in the shadows.

He turned slowly, not sure what he'd heard. It had sounded like something small and metallic falling onto the dirt floor. He checked the area by the furnace to see if a screw had fallen out of the door when he'd opened it but there was nothing there. Glancing around at the small area of floor illuminated by the dim overhead bulb, he couldn't see anything there either.

Leaving the trimmer propped against the wall, he went up to the top step and retrieved the torch. He used it to explore the area near the bureau. Logic told him that if he or Chris had brushed against something that had later fallen to the floor, it had to be in the area in which they'd been standing. But there was nothing on the floor around the bureau.

That left the shadowy corner on the opposite side of the cellar. But neither he nor Chris had been into that area so they couldn't have disturbed something there. When he cast the torch beam in that direction, though, the light reflected off something small and metallic on the floor.

A tiny brass key lying there. He bent down to pick it up, turning it over in his fingers. Where the hell had this come from? He checked the walls for a hook the key might have fallen from but found nothing. And there was no hook on the floor either, so one hadn't fallen off the wall, taking the key with it. There wasn't even a niche in the brickwork where the key might have been resting before it fell. It was as if it had materialised out of thin air.

He went over to the bureau, certain that the

key would fit the brass-decorated locks on the piece of furniture. He inserted it into the top lock, the one that held the foldout writing desk in place, and heard a satisfying click as he turned it. He removed the key and reached for the edge of the desk to unfold it.

"Mike, are you still down there?" Terri's voice shouted from the top of the stairs.

He jumped, startled, and quickly pocketed the key. "I'm here," he said.

"I need some help moving the sofa."

"I'll be there in a minute." He went to open the bureau but then heard his wife coming down the steps. He fumbled the key out of his pocket and relocked the desk before squirrelling it away again.

Terri poked her head around the corner, a look of distaste on her face. "It stinks down here."

Mike just nodded, glad that his face was obscured by the shadows because he was sure he wore a guilty expression. He should have said to Terri, "Hey, look, we found this old bureau and here's the key. Let's see what's inside," but he didn't. He had an inexplicable but undeniable feeling that the key had been dropped onto the cellar floor at that precise moment, when only he'd been down here, because it had been dropped there for him alone.

There was something in that bureau and whatever it was, Mike had an overwhelming compulsion to keep it to himself. He didn't know why, and the feeling was so strong he barely questioned it. But he knew it was important that he keep the contents of the drawer away from his family. It was for their own…

…protection?

He wasn't sure where that thought had come from either, especially when he had no idea what was actually in the drawer. Hell, it might be nothing more than an old paperweight, or an empty snuffbox, or even a rat's nest.

But he knew it wasn't any of those things. He knew there was something in there that he was *supposed* to find. Something important.

How he knew these things, he had no idea but he was as certain of them as he was of the face in the photo on his phone, even if nobody else could see it.

"Are you coming?" Terri asked him. "I need to move some furniture and I can't do it on my own. And then I'm going to turn one of those empty rooms upstairs into a studio."

He glanced at the bureau, his fingers touching the key in his pocket. He could tell her to go ahead, that he'd be there in a minute. Tell her he needed to tend to the fire a little longer.

But the bureau wasn't going anywhere and neither was he. He had plenty of time to open it up and discover its secrets.

"Sure, let's go," he said, smiling at Terri.

6

A WALK IN THE WOODS

July 27th

Jen woke up quickly, fear gripping her mind. She sat up in bed and threw off the covers, disoriented when she didn't recognise the familiar shapes and shadows of her bedroom.

Then she remembered that the room she'd expected to see was in London and they didn't live there anymore. She was in Crow House.

She'd had some kind of nightmare and it had been so bad that she'd woken up in a panic but now she couldn't remember what she'd been dreaming about. The digital clock on her bedside table said it was just after 4 a.m. Through her curtain-less window, she could see the night sky gradually lightening to a slate-coloured morning grey. She could also hear the dawn chorus, a sound she wasn't used to hearing. Not because there weren't birds in London but because she rarely woke up early enough to hear their first songs of the day.

She slipped out of bed and went over to the window. Her bedroom was situated at the rear of the house so she could see the lake and the almost endless sea of trees that reached all the way to the lower slopes of the distant hills.

She'd been in that mass of trees yesterday, wandering aimlessly by the lake when…

She frowned, trying to remember. Something had happened there, something that stayed tantalisingly out of reach of her memory. Had she met someone in the woods? No, that couldn't be it. If she'd met someone, she'd remember it, wouldn't she?

Pushing at the blank space in her memory as if she were poking at a loose tooth with her tongue, she tried to work something loose in her mind, something that might allow her to remember, but the events of yesterday remained mysteriously hidden from her recollection.

All she knew was that something *had* happened during her walk in the woods yesterday.

And that both piqued her curiosity and made her afraid.

Should she go back into the woods and retrace her steps? Try to find out what had happened to her? But how could she retrace her steps if she couldn't remember which direction she'd taken?

And what if she forgot everything again? She might end up at the village, the same as yesterday, knowing nothing more than she knew now.

She thought about that for a moment and then had an idea. She'd take her phone with her and she'd record her walk on video. Then, if she lost her memory again, she could replay the video and it would tell her where she'd been and whom she'd met.

Unsure where that last thought had arisen from, she told herself firmly, "I didn't meet anyone in the woods yesterday."

Yeah, you just keep telling yourself that.

The seed of doubt grew into a fully-grown triffid, complete with tentacles and snapping teeth. Jen tried to tell herself again that if she'd met someone, she'd remember it but the more she thought about it, the more certain she became that she *had* met someone in the woods.

She chased the thought away and grabbed

her phone from the bedside table, making sure it was fully charged.

She'd unpacked most of her clothes yesterday but she ignored the wardrobe and went instead to the boxes stacked in the corner. In one of the boxes, she found her gym clothes and an armband for the phone.

Back in London, she and her friends had gone through a gym phase, spending a couple of evenings a week at a local health club. Most of her friends spent the time working out their glutes and thighs, following videos on YouTube to achieve the "perfect booty." Jen, uninterested in developing her lower half and instead trying to lose a bit of weight, had become hooked on running and while her friends were on the leg machines, she racked up a few miles on the treadmill.

She'd bought the armband so she could listen to her playlists while she ran. That phase of her life had only lasted a couple of months, though, and the armband and gym clothes had been relegated to the back of her wardrobe. Now, she had another use for them.

She slid the black leggings on, along with a sports bra and her running vest. The vest didn't cover her arms, which had been fine for the treadmill but not for walking in the woods where low-hanging branches might scratch her so she threw on an old, black long-sleeved top. Her barely-worn New Balance running shoes lay in the bottom of the box so she fished them out and put them on.

As she was lacing them up, she smiled to herself. Her parents would throw a conniption fit if they found out Jen had been in the woods again but she'd simply say she'd been running by the lake. They couldn't get mad at her for exercising could they? She'd tell them she'd been inspired by the beauty of the countryside.

She strapped the armband to her right arm and put her phone into it. She didn't plug her headphones into it but instead pushed them into the pocket of the leggings. She didn't need them for this trip but wanted to be able to put them on when she returned to the house, making it look as if she'd been wearing them all the time. Not that she expected anyone to be awake when she returned—it was very early after all—but she wanted to be prepared for any possibility.

Congratulating herself on her foresight, she opened the door and crept out of her room. The upstairs landing was illuminated by the pale grey morning light seeping in through the large window and looked otherworldly.

Maybe she should go back to bed and visit the woods later in the day when the sun was up. That would be more sensible than sneaking out at the crack of dawn. But she wanted answers now and had the feeling that if she waited too long, she'd never find them.

The stairs creaked as she stepped onto them and she paused, listening for a sound that might mean Chris or her parents were awake. If her parents found her sneaking out, they'd probably ground her and if Chris woke up, he'd definitely tell on her.

But the house was silent.

She took the remaining steps two at a time until she was standing on the chessboard-patterned tiles in the hallway. Again she paused and again heard no sounds of anyone stirring upstairs.

Satisfied that everyone else in the house was asleep, she went through into the kitchen and to the back door. The key hung on a hook next to the door, a hook that must have been put there by a previous occupant for just that purpose. Jen took the key and unlocked the door before slipping out into the back garden.

A chill hung in the morning air and Jen shivered as she walked across the garden and through the gate. The lake was shrouded in mist. She looked at the woods, which were still dark, and felt a different kind of chill creep up her spine. What had seemed like a good idea when she was safe in her room seemed like a bad idea now that she was actually out here.

A very bad idea.

She was no fan of horror movies but she'd seen enough to know that the people in them always did stupid things like splitting up from the main group, or reading curses from old spell books, or going into creepy woods alone. And those people always ended up dead.

There's nothing to be afraid of. This isn't a horror movie. It'll be daylight soon.

She wondered if she should wait for the dull morning light to brighten into full daylight but she knew that if she waited here too long, her dad might see her. He usually got up in the early hours and went to the bathroom. If he did the same this morning, happened to look out of the window, and saw her standing outside, she'd be grounded faster than she could say, "morning run."

She could prevent that from happening if she just got far enough into the trees that she couldn't be seen from the house. Then she could wait for daylight before going any farther. It wasn't a plan she particularly liked but it was a plan.

Telling herself she only had to go a few feet

into the shadows to be hidden from the bathroom window, she skirted the misty lake and stepped beneath the trees. As she stood in the darkness, she realised she was breathing so heavily that anyone standing hear her would be able to hear her.

Stop that, there's nobody else here. Just the birds and probably a few squirrels. Take a chill pill.

All she had to do now was wait for the sun to come fully up. Then she'd take a walk in the woods, try to remember what happened yesterday, and be back before anyone in the house even knew she was gone. She decided not to start recording the video until she actually went deeper into the woods; the battery on her phone wasn't great, even when fully charged, and the video app would quickly drain it.

Just as she was wondering how long she was going have to wait here and how much daylight was waiting for before she'd dare commence her plan, the saw a light through the trees. It wasn't sunlight, just a small flickering glow in the distance. It was so small, she had to move her gaze away from it and back again to make sure she wasn't seeing things. But it was still there, a tiny flicker of light barely visible in the gloom.

She turned on the video app and began recording, immediately realising she had a problem. The armband kept the phone on the outside of her arm, facing to her right. If she tried to adjust the band so the phone faced forward, it sat in the crook of her elbow, meaning she couldn't bend her arm. So she kept the phone in its original position and twisted her arm, hoping the camera was picking up the light in the distance.

"I guess I should check that out," she whispered loud enough for the microphone to pick up her voice. She wondered if this video might end up on YouTube. What if she discovered a ghost in the woods or something? Her morning walk would go viral and she'd be a star.

The only problem with that scenario was that there were no such things as ghosts. Only her dorky brother believed in those kinds of things. Every time a hoaxer uploaded a video that supposedly showed UFOs, Bigfoot, or the Loch Ness monster, Chris fell for it hook, line, and sinker.

The light in the woods would be something much more mundane than any of Chris's fantasies. Maybe a hiker had left a torch on the ground or the sun was reflecting off a piece of glass or something.

Except there isn't much sun yet, she reminded herself.

A torch then, left behind by a careless hiker.

She walked toward the flickering glow, her running shoes cracking twigs and rustling through the undergrowth, sounding incredibly loud. For a moment, Jen had the terrifying thought that the torch might not have been left in the woods at all. What if someone was standing there, shining a light at her?

That stopped her in her tracks. She froze, hardly daring to breathe while she watched the light for any sign of movement. If someone was holding it in their hand, surely the light would move, unless the person holding it were trying no to move a muscle, just as Jen was doing now.

That didn't really make sense. If they were trying to hide from her, then why shine a light in her direction? Jen took a couple of hesitant steps forward. She wasn't going to call out, "Hello, is anyone there?" like the foolish people in horror movies but she wondered if what she was doing—moving toward the light—was any more sensible. She felt like a moth being drawn toward a flame.

"I'm getting closer," she said for the benefit of her future viewers if this ever made it onto the Net. Daylight was diffusing through the foliage above her now, gradually brightening the woods, chasing away the shadows.

As she got closer, Jen could see that the light

she'd been drawn toward was a candle in the window of an abandoned little house.

It isn't abandoned, she told herself. *Someone lit that candle.*

Sitting next to a huge oak tree, the house had a main floor at ground level and a single room upstairs. The structure was made of wood and had a small porch at the front, overgrown with moss and ivy. The windows were all intact, although the wooden grills that decorated the panes—large diamond patterns on the main window, smaller crisscrossing diagonals on the others—were rotten.

A stone chimney rose from the roof but there was no smoke issuing from it. The place was run-down and overgrown with weeds and if not for the candle flickering in the window, Jen would have assumed the place abandoned. Surely no one could live in such a ramshackle building.

She angled her arm so the phone's camera pointed at her face. "Who lives in a place like this?" she asked.

Stepping up onto the porch and cupping her hands against one of the windowpanes, she peered inside and saw an empty room. There was a dead fireplace on one wall but nothing else in there, other than the candle, which sat on the window cill in a silver holder. The candle, which had probably once been white, was yellowed with age, the holder festooned with cobwebs. Yet someone had lit it and put it in the window for some purpose.

She moved to another window and found another empty room. She was sure those two empty rooms were the extent of the ground floor, which meant that if someone was living here, they must be living upstairs. Jen could see the stairs leading up to the next floor.

She pointed the phone through the windows so the empty rooms would be captured on video.

The little house had a front door whose paint was flaking away like dandruff from a scalp and Jen wondered if she should try to open it but stopped herself as she was reaching for the door handle. She didn't want to go inside the house.

She turned away and stepped off the porch. Whatever had happened yesterday while she was in the woods, she was sure it hadn't involved this little house. She would have remembered this place for sure.

If not the house itself, she would have remembered the huge oak tree that towered next to it. The tree must be at least a couple of hundred years old and wasn't something anyone could forget easily.

As she walked away, feeling more confident now that the woods were getting lighter, she looked back at the house only once.

The candle in the window had been extinguished.

7

THE BOX

Mike woke up at 7 a.m. His alarm wasn't due to go off for another hour but the sunlight streaming in through the window had dragged him from the depths of an unremembered dream. He sat up in bed, knowing there was no way he would get back to sleep now that he was awake.

Terri, seemingly unaffected by the bright morning light, slept soundly next to him. She'd stayed up late last night, working in a painting in her new studio. Mike was glad that at least Crow House could give her a dedicated room for her art, something she never had in the London flat. Maybe it would be enough to eventually win Terri around to liking this place.

He rolled out of bed and quietly put on his jeans and an old Black Sabbath T-shirt before grabbing his phone and switching off the alarm. He went downstairs to the kitchen and turned on the coffee maker. Since it didn't look like he was going to get back to sleep anyway, he might as well load himself with caffeine and seal the deal.

While the pot brewed, he leaned on the worktop, arms folded, peering at the cellar door. Everyone else in the house was asleep, so this might be a good time to go down there and see what was inside that bureau. He still felt that whatever was locked away there was meant for his eyes only but he couldn't explain why. He just knew that if he went down there now, he take a look at what was down there undisturbed by the rest of the family.

Away from prying eyes.

He had no idea where that thought had come from. Terri, Jen, and Chris hardly qualified as "prying eyes." They were his family.

Yet he couldn't deny that he felt a strong urge to keep the contents of the bureau from them.

"It might just be a load of old junk anyway," he told himself as he crossed the kitchen to the cellar door. But he had a strong feeling—so strong it was almost a certainty—that there was something very important down there. He couldn't rationalise that thought nor could he shake it.

He descended the cellar steps quickly, ignoring the torch and feeling around in the darkness at the foot of the steps for the light switch. He found it and the dim bulb brightened slightly, casting a pale yellow glow over everything.

The embers in the furnace burned a subdued orange. The air was warm and smelled of wood smoke. Mike went over to the bureau and fished the key out of his jeans.

He inserted it into the top lock and turned it quickly. The latch opened and he pulled down the foldout writing desk. It was padded with leather and looked—to Mike's untrained eyes at least—to be of high quality.

There was nothing else in the top section of the bureau. Mike closed it up again and locked it before moving down to the drawers. The two small drawers yielded nothing so he quickly relocked them and tried the first of the two large drawers. When he opened it, he found a small, green hardback notebook. He flicked through the pages and saw spidery handwriting but the light in the cellar was too dim to see anything clearly.

He placed the notebook on top of the bureau and relocked the drawer. That left only the bottom drawer to explore. He knew there was something substantial in there because he'd heard it thud against the side of the drawer yesterday. The small notebook couldn't have made such a sound.

He unlocked the drawer and pulled it open. It scraped against its frame, probably the result of the wood warping in the damp cellar, but Mike managed to pull it all the way out with some effort. Sitting inside was a cardboard box, sealed with brown packing tape. He picked it up and placed it on top of the bureau, next to the notebook, before shoving the drawer closed and locking it.

Staring at his treasures—the taped-up cardboard box and the small notebook—he wondered how he was going to inspect them closely without being interrupted. There wasn't enough light down here in the cellar, which meant he'd have to take them upstairs, into the main part of the house. Maybe he could hide them in one of the empty bedrooms. No, that was no good; someone else might stumble across them. He supposed he could leave them down here in the cellar and wait until he got a new bulb but he didn't want to wait that long.

The woods. He could take his treasures into the woods and inspect them there. He could even hide them there if need be. Terri and

Chris were terrified of the woods and wouldn't disturb him there. Jen might decide to take another walk among the trees but he could easily avoid her. Besides, she wasn't awake yet and, assuming her early morning stroll yesterday was an aberration and that she'd now returned to her old habits, wouldn't be awake for a couple more hours.

He put the box under his arm and pushed the notebook into his back pocket before turning off the light and ascending the stairs to the kitchen. Once there, he stopped by the cellar door and listened for any telltale noises that would indicate someone else was awake in the house. The only sound was a slight gurgle from the coffee machine as it dripped the last of the coffee into the pot

Everyone was still asleep.

Deciding to forego his coffee until later, Mike got his boots from the hall and carried them to the back door before sliding his feet into them. For a moment, he saw himself from a birds-eye view, sneaking around the house and keeping secrets from his family. He wondered why he was acting in such a way. But the thought only lasted a couple of seconds and then he was taking the back door key from the hook on the wall and inserting it into the lock.

The door was already unlocked, which he

found strange, as he was sure he'd locked it last night. Reasoning that Terri, Chris, or Jen must have gone out after he'd locked it and left it open when they'd come back in, he slipped out of the house and closed the door behind him.

Despite the early hour, it was already bright and warm outside. When Mike opened the gate and stepped through it, sunlight reflected off the lake, flashing into his eyes as if transmitting a heliographic message. He knew it was a flight of fancy to assume there was meaning in the random flashes of light but standing here alone by the water's edge, it was easy to believe the lake were communicating with him.

He could stand here all day and try to decipher the code being flashed into his mind but his desire to examine the contents of the box under his arm burned bright so he pulled his eyes away from the shimmering water and kept his head down as he marched into the woods. Only when he reached the cool shadows beneath the trees did he raise his head and look around, and he kept his gaze away from the allure of the lake.

Moving deeper into the woods, he looked for a suitable spot to sit down and examine the box's contents. A fallen log would be ideal. He searched in vain for a few minutes and found no log. But he did see something else. In the distance through the trees. A flickering light. It seemed to be a good distance away but because of the gloom it was easily visible.

Mike decided to take a look. If a group of hikers had built a campfire and what he was seeing was the dying embers of that fire, there might also be something to sit on. Just so long as the hikers had moved on. He didn't want to open the box in front of anyone else.

When he got closer to the light source, though, he realised it was a candle in the window of a small wooden house. The house seemed to be mostly a single level structure except for a gable-fronted dormer jutting out from the slanted roof, which suggested an attic room. Mike's curiosity was piqued. Who the hell lived out here in the middle of the woods? Crow House was isolated but at least it had an access road. This place was unreachable except by foot and the building itself looked like it was slowly collapsing.

A tall, ancient oak tree rose from the ground by the house, dwarfing the house with its grandeur.

There were no signs of life other than the candle burning in the window. Mike peered inside and decided that no one lived here after all; the house was devoid of furniture or anything else that would suggest a home.

Then he noticed that the front door was slightly ajar.

He didn't see any reason not to go inside. The place was obviously abandoned, despite the yellowing candle burning in the silver holder. He had no idea why the candle had been placed in the window but it seemed that whoever had put it there, they were long gone now.

So he could use the abandoned house to open the box, inspect its contents, and read the notebook. He could sit on the stairs and take his time. Just as he'd had a gut feeling that the contents of the bureau were for him and him alone, he had an equally strong feeling that the light in the window had been lit just for him, to bring him to the house, the place where he was supposed to open the box and read the notebook.

He knew how crazy that would sound if he voiced it out loud to anyone else but he wasn't going to do that. He was going to keep it to himself.

He pushed through the door and shouted, "Hello?" even though he knew there would be no answer. As expected, the little house remained silent.

Mike blew out the candle. It had done its job

by bringing him here, no need to leave it burning.

It brought me here like a moth to a flame, he told himself before dismissing that thought. Moths that flew to a flame were eventually doomed.

Turning his attention to the interior of the house, he discovered that despite the ramshackle appearance of the place from the outside, it seemed to be structurally sound. There was no dampness on the walls, no cracks running across the ceiling, no subsidence of the wooden floor.

The other thing that was absent here—something that Mike would expect to see in an abandoned building—was any sign of vandalism. In London, a house only had to stand empty for a week or so before squatters and junkies moved in, littering the place with discarded needles, sleeping bags, and graffiti on the walls.

This house was hidden in the woods but he would have expected someone to have found it. The locals must know about its existence yet the black and white floral wallpaper, while aged and faded, was free from spray-painted tags. There was no litter on the floor. It was as if he was the first person to step inside the house since the previous occupants had moved out, whenever that might have been.

The stairs led up to a closed wooden door that had been painted white and when Mike first saw the door, he revised his opinion regarding vandals because there were red marks on the white paintwork that looked like graffiti tags. But when he looked closer, he realised they were carefully painted symbols.

There were three of them and although they seemed to be some sort of magical signs, they were quite unlike the ones Mike had seen carved into the rock by the lake. The first symbol, placed high on the door, was a six-petalled flower within a circle. The next symbol, which had been painted directly beneath the flower design, was of a cross. At the base of the cross were two interlocking triangles. The third symbol depicted two chain links twisted together to form a knot.

The symbols on the rock had been based on pentagrams and therefore recognisable but Mike had never seen symbols like these. The only familiar shape here was the cross, which might suggest that this particular design had a Christian origin. But what did the two interlocking triangles mean?

He decided to look it up online later. One thing he was certain of, though, was that these signs didn't creep him out like the ones at the rock had. In fact, something about them felt strangely comforting.

He tried the door, expecting for some reason that it would be locked. It wasn't. It swung open, revealing a small room with a slanted ceiling formed by the roof of the house. The single window let daylight into the room and that light fell upon the room's only piece of furniture: a metal bed frame.

So someone did live here, Mike thought, *and this was their bedroom*. But when he stepped into the room and took a closer look at the bed, he changed his mind about that. Someone may have lived here but it looked like they'd been kept here against their will.

Attached to the top and bottom of the bed frame were thick chains and iron manacles.

"Either someone went all fifty shades in here or they were being held prisoner," Mike mumbled to himself.

He didn't like the atmosphere in here so he left the room and shut the door. Again, when he saw the symbols that had been painted on the outside of the door, he felt a sense of calmness.

Settling himself on the bottom step, he placed the box on his lap and picked at the packing tape with his fingernail. He soon got the top strip free and pulled it away from the cardboard. It made a ripping sound that sounded very loud in the empty house. Mike rolled the tape into a ball and discarded it before opening the box and looking inside.

The first thing he saw was some sort of white fabric with red designs embroidered into it. The fabric lay over the rest of the contents of the box save for one item: sitting on top of the material was a silver talisman on a fine chain. The talisman was disc-shaped and engraved with a complex design that included concentric triangles, circles, and what Mike assumed were Hebrew letters. He turned the disc over and found the letters *J.C.* scratched into the metal.

He guessed the J.C. who owned this talisman had been related somehow to the E.C. who had carved the initials on the rock by the lake.

He wasn't in the mood to create a story behind the mysterious J.C. or even guess at what the initials stood for. He needed to see what else was in the box.

Removing the embroidered fabric and finding it to be as large as a tightly folded bed sheet, he set it aside, along with the talisman, and delved deeper into the box. His fingers contacted something hard and he pulled out a stack of letters tied tightly together with brown string. The top envelope bore a name and address written in flowing black script.

Jonathan Cain, Esq.
 Crow House
 Matlock
 Derbyshire

That explained the J.C. Jonathan Cain must have been a previous owner of Crow House, perhaps the original owner judging by the yellowing on the envelope and the lilac stamp affixed to its corner. Mike was no philatelist but he recognised Queen Victoria's visage on the stamp, which also bore the price of "one penny" beneath the queen's profile. The postmark was blurry but still legible. *1892.*

Placing the bundle of letters on the step above him, Mike reached into the cardboard box and brought out a small notebook. It was slightly larger than the hardback notebook he'd found earlier and this one was leather-bound. He leafed through a few pages and found neatly flowing handwriting, very different to the spidery scrawls in the smaller notebook.

He assumed the neat handwriting was the work of Jonathan Cain, if only because the leather-bound book had been found in the same box as the letters, and they definitely belonged to Jonathan. So who was the writer of the spidery script in the other notebook?

"All will be revealed in time," he muttered to himself. Surely whoever had written in the little green book would have revealed their name somewhere within the pages.

There was nothing else in the cardboard box. Mike took stock of what he'd found: the embroidered fabric, the talisman, the small green notebook, the larger leather-bound book, and the letters.

Someone had considered these items valuable enough to lock away and hide in the cellar of Crow House. Much of the house's old furniture had obviously disappeared over the years but the bureau had been put into the cellar for a reason, and the cardboard box locked inside its bottom drawer.

There was a story here, among these things. A story from the past. All he had to do was piece it together from the various items.

"Where do I begin?" he asked out loud. The letters were probably the oldest thing here, dating back to 1892, and might be the logical place to start. But the leather-bound book might be older. Mike had no way of knowing until he read it. The green hardback notebook looked like it was the newest thing here, a theory that was probably borne out by the fact he'd found it in a different drawer.

He picked it up, feeling its weight in his hand. If the entries in this notebook were the most recent thing here, then they might shed a light on everything else. Somebody in the recent past could have discovered the meaning of the letters, symbols and talisman and revealed it in the notebook.

Mike opened the cover. The first page had a drawing of a rainbow, made with coloured pencils and beneath that, the words *My Diary by Wendy Maxwell* written in a style of handwriting that suggested someone had taken great care to make it look neat.

The drawing of the rainbow wasn't childish; it looked as if an adult had made it, with precise lines describing the arc of the rainbow and the colours in the correct order. Red, orange, yellow, green, blue, indigo, violet. Mike had been taught a mnemonic in school to remember the order of the colours: Richard Of York Gave Battle In Vain. He wondered if Wendy Maxwell had been taught the same method or if she'd drawn this rainbow from life, perhaps looking out of one of the windows at Crow House.

The next page didn't tell him any more

about the rainbow but it did tell him when this diary had been written. The first entry was headed: *July 25th, 1973.* Beneath the heading, the following words were written in a neat cursive style: *Today we moved into Crow House. It's beautiful! And we even have a lake at the bottom of the garden! Simon and Claire love the house just as much as I do, if that's possible. Our own little slice of heaven.*

Mike frowned at the date on the top of the page. The Maxwell family had moved into Crow House on July 25th, 1973. His own family had moved in on July 25th as well.

Just a coincidence?

What else could it be?

Hadn't the date they'd moved into Crow House been totally random? Mike searched his memory, trying to locate the moment that date had been decided on. He remembered Chris standing in the kitchen of their old London flat saying, July 25th" in what Chris thought was a creepy voice but Mike wasn't sure how that date had been decided upon. At the time, he'd been so distraught over losing his job and having to take a handout from Uncle Rob that he wasn't exactly firing on all cylinders mentally.

Wait a minute. Uncle Rob. When Chris had put on his horror voice and said, "July 25th," hadn't Mike just been on the phone with Rob? And hadn't he just announced to the family in the kitchen that day that they would be moving on the 25^h of July because Rob had just suggested it to him? Yes he was sure of it. The date had been Uncle Rob's idea.

But what did that mean? As far as Mike knew, Rob had never heard of the Maxwells. It had to be a coincidence. What else could it be?

Returning his attention to the diary and thumbing through the pages, he noticed something odd about the handwriting. On the first few pages, the writing was neat, as if it had been laid down with great care. In later pages, it became sloppy, as if Wendy had written those entries hurriedly. Toward the back of the diary, the words were almost illegible, scribbled in a thin, spidery hand.

He reasoned that maybe someone else had written the later entries but found it hard to believe that Wendy Maxwell would let someone else write her diary entries for her. It was more likely that her handwriting, for whatever reason, had declined as time went on, from the neat lettering of the title page to the spidery scrawl found in the later pages.

On impulse, Mike flicked to the very last page to see just how bad her writing had become and was surprised to find a single word scrawled over that page.

Gethsemiel.

He frowned at the word, wondering if the letters actually spelled something else that was lost in the messy way the letters were connected to each other. No, he was sure the word was Gethsemiel.

Flicking back a couple of pages, he found the same single word on those pages too. In fact, that word was the only thing Wendy Maxwell had written on the final twenty pages of the diary. There weren't even any dates for those entries, just that one word scribbled on the page.

Mike put the diary aside. The diary probably wasn't a good place to start after all if the whole thing degenerated into illegible words and nonsense at the end.

Instead of trying to decipher Wendy Maxwell's increasingly spidery writing, he picked up the stack of letters and slid the top one from the stack. He found a single piece of paper within the envelope. Removing and unfolding it carefully, he began to read the neatly flowing script on the page.

8

THE LIFT

"Are you okay? Hello?"

The words came to Jen through blackness. She opened her eyes and felt cool grass on her cheek. For some reason, she was lying on the ground. And someone was talking to her, probably the owner of the black Converse sneakers she could see in her peripheral vision.

She pushed herself up on one elbow and looked into the face of the young man who'd spoken to her. He was maybe nineteen or twenty, with collar-length brown hair, grey eyes, and generous lips. He wore a black *Hollywood Vampires* T-shirt, black jeans, and a concerned look on his face.

"Are you all right?" he asked.

Jen nodded automatically and struggled to her feet, wondering what had happened to her.

The last thing she remembered was the house in the woods, the candle in the window. Now she was lying in a field by the road, the woods behind her. Had she tripped? Why had she tripped? Maybe she'd been running.

"I'm Sam," the young man said as Jen regained her feet. He was easily over six feet tall. "Sam Wetherby. That's my sister, Nancy." He pointed at a grey Volvo parked by the side of the road. Jen could see a young blonde girl of maybe six or seven years old in the passenger seat, face pressed against the window, staring at her.

"I was taking her to her dance class in Matlock," Sam explained, "when we saw you lying here by the side of the road. Are you sure you're all right? Do you want a lift anywhere?"

"I'm not sure," Jen said, looking around at her surroundings. All she could see were fields and trees. "Where am I?"

"About a mile south of Shawby," Sam said. "I can give you a ride into the village if you like."

She thought about that. If she called her dad from the village again, he'd want to know why she'd gone there again. He'd probably be okay about it but Mum could be a pain in the ass sometimes and might even ground her. Her best course of action was to get home before anyone else woke up and sneak back into her bed.

But she didn't want to walk back through the woods. She didn't even know the way home from here. When she looked at the trees behind her, she felt chills run up her arms and back.

"Would you be able to give me a lift back to my house?" she asked Sam. She knew that accepting a lift from a stranger wasn't a wise thing to do but she had no other option. Besides, if Sam had wanted to hurt her, he could have done so already while she was lying on the ground, passed out in front of him. As it was, his face showed concern with no trace of malice. And the fact that his sister was in the car made Jen feel safer too.

"Of course," he said cheerily, "Where do you live?"

"Do you know Crow House?"

Something changed in his face. Jen thought for a moment that he seemed scared but then he regained his former cheery expression. "Of course. Crow House it is." He began toward walk to the Volvo. "Nancy, get into the back seat until we drop off Miss…" He looked back at Jen expectantly.

"My name's Jen," she told him. "Jen Wilson."

"Well it's a pleasure to meet you, Jen Wilson." He went around to the passenger side of the car and held the door open to let Nancy out before gesturing to the now-vacant seat with a dramatic sweep of his arm. "Your carriage awaits."

Jen climbed in, giving him a slight smile. Once she was in the car, she removed her phone from the armband and checked it. It was dead. Running the video recorder drained the battery quickly but the phone had been fully charged when she'd entered the woods. Exactly how long had she been gone from home?

The Volvo's dashboard clock told her it was 7:45. That meant she'd been in the woods for three hours.

"You sure you're okay?" Sam asked her as he pulled onto the road. "You look a bit pale."

"I'm fine," she said. How the hell could she have been wandering around the woods for three hours and have no memory of it? Hopefully the video on the phone would shed some more light on what had happened once she charged it up.

She realised Sam would probably think she was a weirdo if she didn't say more, so she added, "Thanks for the lift. Do you live near here?" It was a lame thing to ask—of course he must live near here—but it was something.

"We live in Shawby with our mum," he said.

"I'm a mechanic at Easton's Garage. Do you know it?"

She shook her head. "We've only been here a couple of days."

"Well anyway, that's where I work. How about you? What brings you to Crow House?"

"We moved here from London," she said. It didn't answer his question but she wasn't going to tell him about her dad losing his job.

"Cool." He went quiet after that, as if he didn't know what else to say, but Nancy filled the silence.

"I'm doing jazz and tap today. Can you dance?"

"No," Jen said. "I'm a terrible dancer." She turned to look at the girl in the back seat. "I bet you're really good, though."

Nancy beamed at her and nodded.

"So," Sam said, "Crow House. What's it like living there? Spooky?"

He was starting to sound like Chris now. What was it with boys and ghosts? "Not really," she said. "It's old but it isn't really spooky."

"Oh." He turned his attention back to the road.

Jen looked at him closely. "Do you know something about the house?"

He shrugged. "I probably shouldn't have said anything."

"No, come one, tell me. What do you know?"

"It's haunted by the souls of dead witches," Nancy said from the back seat.

"What?" Jen asked.

Sam let out a long sigh. "That isn't what I was going to say."

"So what *were* you going to say?"

"Something funny happened there in the seventies, that's all. If this were any other place, like London or Manchester, everyone would have forgotten about it by now. It's only because we live in a tiny village that everyone still talks about it."

"About what?"

Sam seemed to be going through some sort of internal debate for a couple of seconds. Then he shrugged. "I suppose you'll find out about it sooner or later. A family lived in Crow House and the father drowned his wife and daughter in the lake. Afterwards, he told the police that he did it because they were witches."

"That's horrible," Jen said.

"Yeah, and that's not even the weird part," Sam said. "It turns out that in the seventeenth century, that lake was used as a drowning pool."

Jen frowned. "What does that mean?"

"It's where they used to kill witches in the old days," Nancy said. "They threw them in the water and watched them drown. Sometimes they held them underwater with poles until they were dead."

"All right," Sam said, glancing at his sister in the rearview mirror. "That's enough of that."

"Jen asked, so I was telling her," Nancy said.

Jen shivered. "That's creepy. My bedroom looks out over the lake."

Sam looked over at Jen. "Anyway, Nancy's right; that's what a drowning pool was. And then, all those years later, Maxwell killed his wife and daughter in the same way. Weird, huh?"

"Not necessarily," Jen said. "He obviously knew what the lake had been used for in the past and that's why he chose to drown his family. He probably tried to get an insanity plea or something. Was that his name? Maxwell?"

"That's right, Simon Maxwell. And he didn't plead insanity. He insisted that he was completely sane and that his wife Wendy and his daughter Claire were witches who worshipped a demon that lived in the woods. He was ruled insane by the court, though, and ended up in a mental asylum instead of jail."

"So that proves my theory that he knew about the lake's history and used it to get an insanity plea."

"But he insisted he wasn't insane."

"But it was obvious from what he was saying that the judge would think he was. After all, no insane person says they're insane. So Simon Maxwell had to say he wasn't insane so it would appear that he *was* insane. Does that make sense?"

Sam shrugged. "I don't know, maybe. All I know is that people around here avoid that lake and the woods around it." He sighed. "I suppose that to a city girl like you, we must sound like superstitious country bumpkins."

"You said that, not me," Jen told him.

He laughed. "Yeah, well, we do have some silly superstitions, I suppose. I'm sure your house is fine. I didn't mean to scare you or anything."

"You didn't. I don't believe in any of that kind of stuff. My brother, Chris, believes in ghosts and UFOs and everything else but I'm the level-headed one. I take after my dad. He's always talking about what's rational and irrational. He doesn't believe in any weird stuff at all. He's the most rational person in the world."

9

MESSAGES FROM THE PAST

MIKE PUT the first letter aside and reflected on what he'd just read. The letter was from a Doctor Bartholomew Evans in London to Jonathan Cain at Crow House. The tone of writing suggested that the two men were friends and the letter itself was nothing more than good-natured banter between them.

He glanced at the letter and read it again.

18th of May, 1892

Dear John,

. . .

I hope this letter finds you enjoying your new countryside haunt.

Despite my better judgement, I have decided to write you a letter congratulating you on your move to the country. I hope your new home, Crow House, is comfortable and accommodating for Mary, Elizabeth, and, of course, yourself.

Although I will add that some of your old friends here in the city have placed wagers on how long it will be before you decide you hate the country and return to London. I, of course, would never place such a bet and I told everyone that I am fully confident that you will love your new surroundings so much that we'll never see hide nor hair of you in London again.

I joke, of course. I actually took a wager with the rest of them and would like to inform you that if you choose to eschew the countryside and return to London in precisely two months' time, I stand to win quite a lot of money.

Please write me at your earliest convenience and let me know how you are getting on. If nothing else, a continued communication with London should keep you free from the loneliness that is sure to come with living in an isolated house in the damnable countryside.

. . .

Your friend,
  Bart

Mike removed the string from around the remaining letters in the stack and checked the handwriting on the envelopes. They all seemed to be from Dr. Evans. He removed the envelope from the bottom of the stack, reasoning that it was probably the latest communication from the doctor since the earliest letter had been on the top. He took the letter from the envelope and began to read.

25th of July, 1892

Dear John,

I hope this letter finds you well.

Your latest communication, which I received this morning, has brought me to my writing desk directly. Your earlier letters convinced me that Mary was suffering from some strange malady but having read today's communication, I believe it is you who may require the attention of a professional.

Unfortunately, the help you need is beyond the scope of my medical training as I feel an alienist is required in this situation. Yes, John, I am saying that the problem is within your own head. I implore you to come down to London where I can introduce you to a friend of mine who possesses outstanding credentials in the field of curing illnesses of the mind.

Do this, I beg of you, for your own sake and the sakes of both Mary and Elizabeth. Otherwise, I dread to think where all this will end. Your talk of occult books and practices has me worried, I will admit to that.

John, please come and see me immediately. Who knows, perhaps being back in the city will be all that is required to get you on an even keel and perhaps the alienist will not be required after all.

I fear you have been infected with the superstitious nonsense that is the bread and butter of the country folk. I told you no good would come from moving to such an isolated place. Witchcraft indeed! A good spell (excuse the pun) in the city will cure you of such notions.

I hope to see you soon, my old friend.

Sincerely,

Bart

Mike pondered over the differences in tone between this letter and the other. The first was light, friendly, humorous even, yet the letter from the bottom of the stack seemed to be a warning written in all seriousness.

The time that had passed between the writing of the letters was no more than two months. What had happened in that short time for the doctor to go from joking with Jonathan Cain about living in the country to issuing a dire warning regarding his friend's mental health?

Unfortunately, Mike only had one side of this epistolary conversation: the letters from the doctor to Cain. There wouldn't be any copies of the letters Cain had sent to the doctor so Mike was going to have to piece the clues together from what little he had.

Maybe one of the letters in the middle of the pile would reveal what it was that Cain had written about. There might be a mention of Mary's "strange malady" that Dr. Evans had referred to. It was clear that Cain had mentioned witchcraft at some point but in what context? Had he believed Mary to be a witch? If so, why?

The sudden ringing of his phone made Mike jump. The digital ringtone sounded so loud in the empty house. It also sounded out of place, as if the modern world were intruding into a place it didn't belong.

Mike checked the screen. It was Terri. She was probably wondering where he was. "Hey," he said. "What's up?"

"Mike, where are you? Are you with Jen?"

"With Jen? What do you mean?"

"I mean she isn't here. Is she with you?"

"No," he said, getting up off the step, the letters tumbling from his lap to the floor.

"Well wherever she is, she's taken her phone with her this time but every time I ring it, I just get her voicemail."

"I'll be right there," Mike said. He ended the call and quickly shoved the letters back into the box, along with the leather-bound book and the diary. He placed the large piece of embroidered fabric on top and was about to place the talisman on top of that when, on a whim, he decided to wear it. He fastened the silver chain behind his neck and looked down at the intricately carved disc that now lay against his chest. He decided he liked it and stuffed it underneath his Black Sabbath T-shirt. Now only he knew it was there, which seemed important for some reason.

He needed to take the box back to Crow House without it being seen but he wasn't sure how he was going to do that. The only other option was to leave the box here and come back for it later. He didn't like the idea of that because anyone could stumble upon this house in the woods and get inside. If someone else found the box, they might steal it and then he'd never see it again.

He weighed up the two alternatives. If Terri saw him walking into Crow House with a box under his arm, she'd ask him what was inside. Mike still had an unshakeable urge to keep the contents of the box a secret. On the other hand, if he left it here, it might vanish forever.

Deciding he'd have to risk getting the box into Crow House undiscovered, he picked it up and left the small house, closing the front door behind him. As he walked past the huge oak, he briefly contemplated burying the box beneath it, in the ground between the tree's thick roots, but then realised he'd have to dig it up every time he wanted it. That was no good. His best plan was to get the box back into the bureau and lock it away. Then, he could access it whenever he needed it.

He frowned at his own thoughts. Needed it? The box contained some old letters from the nineteenth century, a leather-bound book that was probably just as old, a diary from the 1970s, and a piece of cloth embroidered with weird symbols. What could he possibly need among those things?

But something told him that everything in the box was important, that he'd need all of those items in the near future. In fact, he had an unshakeable feeling that they might mean the difference between life and death.

He shook his head at that. He felt as if two parts of his mind were at war: the rational part that he'd always prided himself on following and a deeper, as yet undiscovered, part that was powered by intuition and other unseen forces.

At the moment, those two parts of himself were vying for control, making Mike feel giddy, as if he were on a rollercoaster. His rational mind questioned his actions. Hiding the box from his family, stealing away to an abandoned house in the woods, becoming interested in something that had happed at Crow House over a century ago.

Yet the deeper part of his mind told him that all these things were normal. In fact, it told him that they were important for the safety of his family.

He had no idea what that meant but couldn't deny the strong subconscious messages that seemed to well up from the very depths of his being.

So he hatched a plan to get the box into Crow House without Terri seeing it. When he reached the back garden, he'd ring her and ask her to fetch something from the Sportage for him. It didn't matter what, just as long as it got her out of the house while he crept in through the back door and sneaked down to the cellar to lock the box safely away.

But as he reached into the back wall and was about to take out his phone, it began to ring. It was Terri.

As soon as he picked up, she began speaking. "I don't know where you are but you need to get back here now. A car has just pulled up at the gate and Jen is inside it with a man."

"Nearly there," he told her. "You go out and see who it is and I'll join you in a minute."

She hung up on him. Mike pushed through the back gate and crossed the garden quickly. He opened the kitchen door and stuck his head inside to make sure the coast was clear. He heard the front door open and Terri's voice saying, "Where the hell have you been, Jen?"

He slipped inside and descended the stairs to the cellar as quietly as he could before unlocking the bureau and placing the box in the bottom drawer. Then he locked everything up again and went back upstairs to see what all the fuss was regarding Jen.

By the time he got to the front door, he could see a grey Volvo idling by the gate and Jen climbing out of it, thanking a young man behind the wheel. Terri stood at the gate, arms folded with a look of thunder on her face, and Chris was sitting on the front step watching everything with a bemused expression.

"That didn't take her long, Dad," he said when he saw Mike. "She's got a boyfriend already."

"Don't be silly, Chris," Mike said, striding down to the gate.

By now, Terri was at the car, talking to the young man through his open window. Jen was rolling her eyes and stalking toward the house.

As the car pulled away, Terri grabbed Jen's arm and said, "Just what do you think you're doing accepting lifts from strangers?"

"It's fine, Mum." Jen looked bored of the conversation already. "He's a nice guy. I fell over and he helped me get home."

"What do you mean you fell over? Where were you?"

"Just up the road," Jen said, waving her arm vaguely in the direction of the disappearing Volvo. "I was jogging. I tripped and Sam just happened to be driving by so he offered me a lift."

"And you accepted? Jen, he's a total stranger. He could have been an axe murderer for all you knew, yet you got into a car with him. We didn't bring you up to make stupid mistakes like that."

"It wasn't a mistake and he's not an axe murderer. His six-year-old sister was in the backseat, for God's sake." She stormed past Mike, across the garden and in through the open front door.

"And why the hell were you jogging along a lonely country road at this hour of the morning?" Terri shouted after her. "You never went jogging in London."

"I thought that was the point of living in the countryside," Jen shouted back from inside the house, "To live a healthier lifestyle."

"No," Terri shouted at the house. "The point is we don't have a choice." Her voice wavered and tears welled in her eyes. "We don't have a choice," she repeated softly, as if to herself.

Mike went to her and put his arms around her gently. Terri buried her head against his shoulder and cried softly.

10

PLAYBACK

JEN SLAMMED the bedroom door behind her and collapsed onto the bed, staring up at the ceiling as her mind raced over the past few minutes. Why was her mum such a pain in the ass? Nobody had wanted to move out here from London and it was stressful, Jen got that, but she, dad, and even Chris had gotten on with it whereas her mum was either moping around the house all the time or hulking out at every little thing.

Sam was a nice guy and Jen didn't appreciate her mother having a word with him after he was kind enough to drop her off at home. She wasn't exactly sure what her mum had said but it couldn't be anything good and now Sam would probably steer clear of Jen forever.

For some reason, that upset her more than

she'd expected. She had no friends her in Derbyshire and Sam had been really nice and easy to talk to. The fact that he was good-looking didn't hurt either. She could see herself getting to know him, going out with him for walks, picnics, or whatever the hell people did for fun around here.

But now her mum had ruined it. Word would probably get around the village that the Wilson family living at Crow House was a family of weirdos. The mother was the type of person who told someone off just for giving her daughter a lift home. Jen would become a pariah.

In London, she'd been one of the popular girls with lots of friends and boys hanging on her every word. Out here, she was nobody. Just a scared girl who passed out in front of the first boy she met out while she was out jogging.

Except she hadn't been jogging when she'd passed out; she'd been running. From something in the woods. She was sure of it.

Fishing the dead phone out of her pocket, she rolled over and reached across the nightstand for the charger. Once the phone was plugged in, it shouldn't be long before it had enough juice to play the video she'd taken in the woods.

She put the device on charge and rolled

onto her back to stare at the ceiling again. She hadn't noticed before but there was a dark stain on the plaster up there, as if the area may have been damp at some time in the past and no one had bothered to repaint it.

The stain looked like a girl's face staring down at Jen from the ceiling. Not in a malicious way or anything like that but as if the girl were simply observing Jen dispassionately.

Jen closed her eyes and then opened them again to see if the stain would look like something else this time—a dog or a flower maybe—but the face remained.

She shrugged. It didn't freak her out or anything like that and she knew it was just her mind misinterpreting the random pattern of lines but the longer she looked at the stain, the more certain she was that it formed the face of a girl. The stain-girl had long hair that fell over one half of her face, obscuring it. Only one half of her nose and mouth and only one eye were visible. And that one eye regarded Jen with no emotion.

"Of course it doesn't have any emotion," Jen said to herself softly, "it's just a stain on the ceiling." She rolled over to check the phone. The screen displayed a battery icon and a lightning bolt, telling Jen that it was charging but not ready to be switched on yet.

Jen groaned and rolled over to look up at the stain again. "What are you staring at?" she asked it before groaning again, this time at herself. If her friends could see her now, talking to a patch of damp ceiling, they'd think she was crazy. Hell, maybe she would go crazy living out here so far from the city. Maybe she needed to live in a busy city to stay sane. She certainly needed friends. Maybe even a boyfriend. But now Mum had blown any chance of that ever happening here.

She rolled onto her side to check the phone again. It was finally booting up. When the home screen appeared, she touched the video recorder app and waited for her video to appear. When it finally did, the timer showed that she'd managed to record 32 minutes of video before either the battery had died or the storage space on the phone had been filled.

Jen rolled onto her stomach and rested the phone on her pillow before pressing play. At first, it was hard to see what the camera was pointing at but then the tiny light in the distance came into focus.

"I guess I should check that out," she heard her own voice say. As she walked toward the house, the shot became erratic; it swung with her arm movements, making the trees appear to glide back and forth. She could hear her own footsteps crunching over twigs and leaves and then her voice saying, "I'm getting closer."

The camera swung around and the little house in the woods appeared, framed perfectly in the shot. Then the camera pointed up at her face and she said, "Who lives in a house like this?" The shot from below wasn't flattering at all. Jen could see up her own nostrils, which wasn't a view she'd ever post on the Net. Oh well, a bit of editing would sort that out.

The video showed the house again, this time a shot through the windows. Then it swung erratically again as Jen walked away from the house.

She began to concentrate on the video she was watching more closely now. This was as far as she could remember. Everything the phone captured from this moment on had somehow vanished from her mind.

For at least ten minutes, there was nothing except more trees and the sound of her footsteps as she walked deeper into the woods. She was beginning to think the video hadn't captured anything interesting at all when the camera suddenly halted.

Video-Jen whispered, "Did you hear that?"

Jen turned up the volume on the phone. She hadn't heard anything at all.

"It sounded like someone speaking," Video-Jen said. There was a note of fear in her voice.

Why can't I remember any of this? If I heard someone in the woods, I should be able to remember it. What's happening to my memory?

Video-Jen took a couple of steps forward. As she did so, the crunching of leaves underfoot sounded incredibly loud. Something flashed across the screen like a lens flare. Whatever it was, it must have been something the camera had picked up but that Jen hadn't seen because she was just standing totally still now, not moving, not speaking. The only thing Jen could hear on the video was the sound of her own breathing.

"What are you doing?" she asked her video-self in frustration. "Don't just stand there. Find out who's talking or get out of there."

The microphone picked up a sound like a low rumble. It sounded distorted, causing static on the audio.

When it stopped, Video-Jen still had not moved but suddenly, she spoke. A single word. "Yes."

Jen frowned at the phone. "What? Who are you talking to?" She couldn't see anything other than the trees that had been to her right as she'd stood motionless in the woods.

More static.

"Of course I can," her video-self said. All trace of fear had gone from her voice. Now, she sounded monotone, with barely any inflection at all, like when people in old movies pretend to be hypnotised.

Then the camera began to move again. Her video-self was walking very slowly, her arm movements so minimal that the camera was almost steady. But all it showed were the trees on her right, gliding past as she walked to God-knew-where.

"Turn the camera around," she told her video-self but the shot remained steady, showing nothing more than the trees.

The low, static-ridden rumble sounded again and then Jen heard her own voice on the video again. "The sisters."

"The sisters? What the hell are you talking about? Who are you talking to?" She sat up on the bed, so frustrated with her past self that she wanted to throw the phone out the window. What had she been doing in the woods? Someone had obviously been speaking to her but the only thing the phone had picked up was a rumble and a burst of static. And the most burning question, the one that niggled away in her mind was: Why couldn't she remember any of this?

On the screen, the trees had disappeared

and now she could see the shoreline of the lake. The camera shifted and Jen wondered if her video-self was now kneeling at the water's edge. The ground was very close-up in the shot. It looked like she was kneeling on a large flat rock. Why would she even do that?

A couple of minutes went by and the shot remained almost totally still. What had she been doing, kneeling there and staring into the water or something?

The mic picked up a new sound, the loud splintering of wood and rustling of leaves. It sounded as if something large were coming through the trees.

More rumble and static.

Then her own voice, slightly panicked now. "It's coming." The video spun suddenly as her video-self got to her feet in a hurry and then began running through the trees. Jen could barely watch the violent motion of the trees blurring past the camera without feeling nauseous. She could still hear something crashing through the trees and now also her own breathing, hard and fast. She realised that it wasn't only her video-self panting; she was doing the same thing right now, willing herself to flee whatever was coming through the woods.

"Run," she whispered urgently.

Then the video ended.

Jen sprung up from the bed and paced the room, full of unspent, adrenaline-fuelled, energy.

How long had she been running? She'd left the house at 4:30 a.m. and the video had recorded 32 minutes, which meant she'd started running at around 5 a.m. Yet Sam had found her passed out on the ground almost three hours later. She couldn't have been running all that time, it wasn't possible, not for her. She was relatively fit but she was no marathon runner.

So where had she been? Why couldn't she remember?

Her legs felt weak and shaky. She got onto the bed and lay looking up at the stain-face on the ceiling. "What the hell was that thing in the woods?" she asked aloud.

The face had no answers. It simply stared down at Jen with a single, emotionless eye.

11

SPIRIT BOARD

July 28th

It wasn't until later afternoon the following day that Jen plucked up enough courage to approach Chris's room. What she was about to do would be seen, in Chris's eyes, as an admission that she believed in ghosts.

Since viewing the video of herself, she'd spent most of her time examining those beliefs. Until now, she'd been sure they were either the result of over-active imaginations or hoaxes that were created to get views on the Net.

She couldn't deny what was happening to herself, though, and she had proof that it wasn't her imagination playing tricks on her. The video showed her doing some weird stuff; stuff that she had no memory of doing.

The conversation she'd had with Sam had constantly resurfaced in her thoughts. The lake had been a drowning pool for witches. Simon Maxwell had killed his wife and daughter here. Nancy Wetherby had told her that the house was haunted by the souls of dead witches.

Jen had concluded that although she still didn't believe in ghosts, there was undeniably something strange going on here and there might be a certain tool she could use to get more information. Chris might know how to make that tool. Hell, he might even have one.

She knocked on his door.

"Come in," he called.

Jen opened the door and stepped inside. She'd expected her brother to be gaming or surfing the Net but he was lying on the bed reading a book called *Bigfoot: Government Experiment Gone Wrong?* He put the book down as Jen entered the room and asked, "Hey, what's up?"

She hesitated. She knew what she wanted to ask him but wasn't sure how she was going to do it without sounding ridiculous. "You believe in ghosts, right?" Ugh. Dumb question. Of course he believed in ghosts and he knew that she knew that.

He arched an eyebrow and said, "There are more things in heaven and earth, Horatio, than are dreamt of in your philosophy."

She sighed. "There's no need to quote Shakespeare at me. A simple yes or no would be great."

He eyed her suspiciously. "Yes, you know I do. Why?"

"Have you ever thought about making a Ouija board?"

His suspicion was replaced with enthusiasm. "Thought about it? I've done it. Scott Jones and I made one a couple of years ago. Scott wanted to contact his dead grandfather because he thought the old man had hidden some money away somewhere and Scott wanted to get his hands on it."

He jumped up from the bed and went over to a stack of boxes in the corner of the room. After a couple of minutes rummaging around inside one of them, he brought out a tile of wood that had the alphabet, numbers, "Yes," "No," and "Goodbye" carved into its surface. The edges were decorated with swirls and stars and a sun and moon.

"Wow," Jen said, "that looks really nice."

"We made it in Woodworking class," he told her.

"Do you have the pointer thing?"

"You mean the planchette," he said, reaching into the box and bringing out a wedge-shaped piece of wood with a small round window set the pointed end. Chris's suspicion returned and he narrowed his eyes. "Why are you asking about Ouija boards?"

She shrugged. "I'm interested, that's all. Does this one work?"

It was Chris's turn to shrug. "Nah, I don't think so. Me and Scott tried it out but he never did contact his grandfather or find the money. The board didn't actually do anything. After a while, I made the planchette move just to make Scott feel better but I couldn't tell him where his grandfather's treasure was, of course, so he got bored with it."

"Oh cool," she said, not really listening. "Can I borrow it?"

He brought the planchette up to his mouth as if it were a microphone and spoke in a sports commentator's voice. "Ladies and gentlemen, history is being made here today as Jen Wilson is going to use a Ouija board. Has she finally admitted that her brother Chris was right about ghosts all along?"

"Shut up," she told him. "I didn't say I was going to use it. I just want to borrow it."

He held the planchette in front of her as if he were interviewing her. "Jen Wilson, can you explain to our viewers why you wish to borrow a Ouija board if you aren't going to use it? It serves no other purpose at all. Indeed, its only function is to contact the dead."

"Forget it," she said, pushing his hand away and turning toward the door.

"Wait, wait, I can help you," Chris said, getting in her way. "Just let me in on whatever it is you're doing, okay? Tell me about the ghost."

"There is no ghost."

"There has to be, otherwise you wouldn't want to borrow a Ouija board. We both know you don't believe. You're a cynic, like Dad. So what changed your mind?" He narrowed his eyes again. "You've had some sort of experience, haven't you?"

"Get out of my way." She pushed him aside and left the room. She should have known that asking her little brother for anything would be a mistake. And thinking she'd get answers from a Ouija board was stupid. Who was she hoping to contact, the witches who had been drowned in the lake? The mother and daughter who had been killed here in the seventies? What the hell had she been thinking? Shaking her head in disbelief at her momentary lapse of reason, she returned to her room and closed the door.

"The solution to the problem is simple," she

told herself as she paced back and forth. "I'll just stay away from the woods. I don't know what happened there this morning and maybe I don't need to know. I'll just stay away and it will never happen again."

She wasn't going to be like those dumb actors in horror movies who kept going back to the haunted house, or the pit where the demon lived, or whatever. She was going to act sensibly.

But what if it isn't only the woods that are haunted but this house too? This was where the Maxwells lived, where Simon Maxwell went crazy.

"Stop it," she told herself. "Don't think like that. Whatever happened to you, it happened in the woods, not in the house. The house is fine."

She lay on the bed and looked up at the face on the ceiling. For some reason, she found comfort in the face's unemotional, single-eyed stare.

As Jen's gaze traced the lines that made up the girl's face, her lids became heavy and her body felt as if it were sinking into the bed. She closed her eyes and let her thoughts drift.

Moments before sleep dragged her into a world of dreams, Jen opened her tired eyes and watched as the face detached itself from the ceiling and slowly drifted down toward her.

12

MIDNIGHT

Mike crept out of bed at midnight. He'd been unable to sleep, lying in the dark, listening to Terri breathing deeply beside him and his thoughts had constantly returned to the letters Jonathan Cain had received from Dr. Evans.

Now, as Crow House slept, Mike felt determined to find out more about the communication between Cain and the doctor. Something had happened here a long time ago that Mike felt still had a hold on the house even now, as if a seed planted a century earlier had sprouted tendrils that reached into the present day.

How the touch of those tendrils would affect his family, he had no idea, but he believed the answer was hidden somewhere in the letters and writings he'd locked in the cellar.

After quietly putting his jeans and T-shirt

on so as not to wake Terri, he left the bedroom and felt a chill as he stepped onto the dark landing. Despite the warmth of the day, the house felt like a freezer. Maybe he should have put more wood in the furnace when he'd been in the cellar earlier but at the time, he'd been focused on squirrelling the box away and nothing else.

The stairs creaked as stepped on them. When he was all the way down, the hallway tiles cold beneath his feet, he listened for the sound of any movement upstairs. All was quiet. Everyone was still asleep. He slipped into the kitchen and, without bothering to pic up the flashlight at the top of the cellar stairs, descended into the pitch-black cellar.

He found the light switch and clicked it on, bringing the weak bulb to life. There wasn't enough light to read by so he planned to retrieve the box from the bureau and take it upstairs. Once there, he could sit at the kitchen table beneath the fluorescent lights and read at his leisure.

The bureau key was still in his jeans pocket so he got it out and opened the bottom drawer. The box was sitting exactly where he'd left it, waiting for him. He took it up to the kitchen and switched on the fluorescents that ran along the ceiling. They stuttered for a few seconds before bursting into life and illuminating the room with stark white light.

Mike sat down at the kitchen table and opened the box. Digging past the embroidered fabric, he found the letters and brought them out of the box, setting them on the table and pushing the box out of his way. For now, he was only interested in the letters.

Since he'd already read the letter at the bottom of the stack, as well as the one from the top, he selected one from the middle and opened it.

21st of June, 1892

Dear John

I hope that you, Mary, and Elizabeth are well. Of the matter you mentioned concerning Mary, I don't know what to say, old chap. Isn't it understandable that a woman living in the countryside might grow to love nature?

I don't understand it myself, of course, but I am given to understand that some people enjoy nothing more than spending time in the woods. As you said, this is out of character for Mary but since she has spent all of her life in London until recently, it is probable that her interest in the countryside has always been a part of her character but has only now been able to blossom.

You sounded most concerned about the time she spends in the woods so I ask you to elucidate on this matter, as you did not fully explain your worries.

As for life here in the city, all is well. My practice is ticking over as always and Lydia is in good health for a change. Perhaps some country air would do her good, as the grime of the city seems to settle on her lungs most readily.

Anyway, my friend, try to relax where your wife is concerned. Like you, she has experienced a major change in her life moving to the country and being one of the fairer sex, she may very well take some time to adapt to her new circumstances. As long as she is getting your meals on the table at the appointed times and caring for young Elizabeth, I would not worry too much if I were you.

Write soon, old chap. I look forward to hearing from you soon.

Your good friend,
  Bart

Mike put the letter down, wondering what

Jonathan Cain's concerns had been regarding his wife Mary spending time in the woods. Unfortunately, Cain hadn't explained those concerns fully, even to his friend. Maybe in a later letter...

He took the next letter from the stack and opened it, hoping to find the reason for Cain's concern.

7th of July, 1892

Dear John

I hope this letter finds your family, and particularly Mary in better health.

Her lapses of memory, as described in your most recent letter, are concerning indeed. If she is walking alone in the woods and cannot later recall what she did there or where she went, the situation is most alarming. What if she were to wander away and get lost? I urge you to put a stop to her rambling and find help for her. The lost mind is one that needs immediate attention.

This malady of hers sounds strange indeed. There are probably no competent doctors anywhere in the region of Crow House so you must bring her to London and I shall personally ensure she receives the best care available.

You wrote that she seems obsessed with returning to the woods, even though she cannot explain why she has such a compulsion. I fear she has a disease of the mind that can only be treated by an alienist. Bring her to London, my friend. How is Elizabeth dealing with all of this? It can't be easy on her to have a mother in such a state. I fear for the child.

In fact, I fear for all of you. This move to the country was obviously ill advised. You said in your letter that you feel all alone out there, isolated as you are, so do something about it and return to civilisation! The country is meant for country folk and you are much more civilised than those backwards people. You belong here with a more refined class of people, such as your friends, who miss you dearly.

If I do not hear from you within due course then I shall come up there to fetch you myself. Actually, that is not such a bad idea. Perhaps Lydia and myself should come to Derbyshire and pay you a visit. Only for a couple of days, of course, but long enough for me to get the measure of Mary's illness.

What say you?

Your friend,
Bart

. . .

Mike put the letter back into its envelope and then returned it to the stack. So Cain had convinced Bart that Mary was ill but later, the doctor had revised his opinion and concluded that it was Cain himself who needed medical help. Again, Mike wished he could see Cain's letters, the ones the doctor was replying to. Trying to piece the story together from just the doctor's letters involved too much guesswork.

He leaned back in the chair, glanced over at the window, and started in shock. Because the lights in the kitchen were so bright and it was so dark outside, the windows had become almost mirror-like, reflecting the interior of the room in which Mike sat.

In that reflection, he saw himself sitting at the table and the bearded man he'd seen in the bathroom and in the window standing directly behind him.

Mike turned around in his seat, expecting to see the man standing there but the kitchen was empty. He turned his head to glance at the reflection in the window again and clearly saw the man stepping closer to his chair.

Scrambling to his feet, Mike faced the empty kitchen and shouted, "Get away from me!"

Even though he was alone in the room, he felt something touch his forehead, as if someone had pressed the tip of their finger against his flesh. Panicked, he cast a sideways glance at the window and saw that the bearded man was indeed touching him with a single finger.

Mike whimpered as he felt every muscle in his body tighten into some kind of paralysis. He couldn't move, could only breathe in quick, panicked gasps.

In the reflection, the man leaned in closer. Mike heard a cold voice whisper into his ear. "Remember me."

Then everything went black.

13

THE ARGUMENT

THE FIRST THING he became aware of was Terri's voice calling his name over and over. Then he felt hands grabbing his shoulders and shaking him. At first he wondered if it was the ghost shaking him but then realised it was Terri.

He opened his eyes. He was lying on the kitchen floor beneath the bright kitchen lights. The bearded man was gone.

"Oh, thank God!" Terri cried. "Are you okay? What happened? We've called an ambulance."

Mike got to his feet, feeling absolutely fine. Jen and Chris were standing close to Terri, all three of them wearing identical worried looks on their faces. "No ambulance," he said. "I just…fell over."

"Are you sure?" Terri asked. "Maybe you should get checked over."

"I'm fine," he told her. "Cancel the ambulance."

"I'll do it," Jen said, rolling her eyes. Now that she knew her father wasn't in any real danger, the concerned look had disappeared from her face. She began jabbing at her phone and left the kitchen.

"I heard you shouting," Terri told Mike.

"Oh, that was nothing. I just shouted as I fell over, that's all."

She pointed at the box and the stack of letters on the table. "And what's all this?"

Mike cursed inwardly. These items from the past were no longer his alone to examine, no longer his secret. "Just some old stuff I found in the cellar."

She stepped closer to the table and picked up the stack of letters, inspecting one of the envelopes. "Wow, these really are old. Who was Jonathan Cain?"

"He lived here in the late 1800s."

"And these were in the cellar?"

He nodded, trying to seem nonchalant about the items so that she might lose interest in them. "Yeah, they were inside a bureau. They're just junk really."

Chris looked accusingly at him. "Dad, you

said we shouldn't open the bureau because it didn't belong to us."

"No, I didn't. You wanted to bust it open and I said we shouldn't do that. I found the key."

Chris nodded slowly. "And you didn't bother to tell me. We found that bureau together. I should have been there when you opened it."

"It was hardly anything exciting, Chris, just a bunch of old letters."

"That's not the point. You still should have told me when you found the key."

"Okay, I'm sorry. The next time I find a key to an old piece of furniture, I'll be sure to let you know."

"There's no need to talk to him like that," Terri said.

Mike threw up his hands. "Anyone would think I'd found the lost Ark of the Covenant down there. It's just some old letters."

Terri plucked a letter from its envelope and unfolded it. "What's in them? Anything interesting?"

"Not really," Mike said. He watched her as she read the letter, feeling that she was intruding into his space. He knew he had no claim to the letters or their contents but he was still sure they had been meant for him and him alone. The key to the bureau had been dropped onto the floor, seemingly out of nowhere, for him to find. Not Terri. Not Chris. Not Jen. Him.

Terri frowned at the letter in her hands. "It says here that Jonathan Cain thought his wife, Mary, was a witch." She held the letter up so Mike could see the elegant script. "The doctor is telling him not to be so ridiculous but it sounds like Cain was sure she was a witch because she spent so much time in the woods." She cast a glance at the dark window and shivered. "I told you there was something weird about those woods."

"Don't be silly," Mike said. "People were more superstitious in those days. Mary probably just liked to take walks by the lake. She probably wanted some peace and quiet. Hell, maybe she needed to get away from her husband. It sounds like he was a nutter." He felt a pang as he said those words because he was now sure it was Jonathan Cain's ghost who had given him the key to the bureau and was somehow attempting communication with him.

Remember me.

"Or maybe she really was a witch," Chris said, taking a few steps toward the table. "This is Internet gold. A haunted house. Letters in the cellar. A witch. I need to get this stuff onto my website. What's in the box, Dad?"

"Nothing of any interest," Mike said. "And you 're not putting anything on the Net. We should all go back to bed. It's the early hours of the morning for Christ's sake."

"You're the one who shouted and woke everyone up." Chris opened the box and took out the piece of fabric. His eyes widened when he saw the symbols embroidered into it. "Hell yeah, this is witchcraft. Or the occult. Or something."

Mike tried to grab the fabric from his son but Chris held onto one corner of it and it began to unfold. It was as large as a bed sheet and as it unfolded, more symbols came into view, as well as dark stains on the white material.

"Is that blood?" Chris asked, dropping his corner of the fabric as if he expected the stains to creep across the material and touch him.

The dark stains spread across the fabric from the four corners and they did look like very old, dried blood. Mike thought the dark pattern formed the outline of a person and he was instantly reminded of the Shroud of Turin. Was that what this piece of fabric was: a shroud decorated with occult symbols?

"Mike, I don't like this," Terri said,

concerned. "What is that thing doing in our house?"

He shrugged. "It was in the cellar."

"Why has no one gotten rid of it?"

"I told you, it was locked away."

"Well now it's going to be thrown away. Take it out to the wheelie bin."

"No," he said.

She looked at him, shocked. "What do you mean "no"?

He began to refold the shroud. "This is a piece of history. We can't just throw it out."

"History? It looks like someone bled out on it."

Jen came into the room, sliding her phone into the pocket of her dressing gown. "The ambulance is cancelled. What's everyone shouting about?" Her eyes were drawn to the shroud and when she saw it, her face paled. "No," she whispered, her gaze turning fearful. "No, no!" She turned and fled the room. Mike heard her running upstairs and then a door slam shut up there.

"See what you've done now?" Terri said, pointing an accusatory finger at him. "I want that thing out of the house. Now!" She left the room and went upstairs, presumably to placate Jen.

Chris looked at Mike. "What are we going to do, Dad?"

"You're going to go to bed."

"Oh, come on. I'm on your side. We can't just throw this stuff away. It's a piece of history and it's cool. Do you think there was really a witch who lived here?"

"Bed, Chris. Now."

Chris threw his arms up in mock surrender and made for the door. "Okay, okay, I'm going. But please, Dad, don't get rid of anything. I think there's more going on in this house than any of us realise and we might need that stuff to find out what happened here in the past."

Mike eyed his son closely. "What's that supposed to mean? Have you seen something strange?"

"No, not me," Chris said as he left the room.

Mike watched him go and then turned back to the table. He had no intention of getting rid of anything. He was just going to have to hide the box in a place where no one would find it. Locking it in the bureau was no good because he had no doubt Chris would look there first. There weren't any other places in the house where Terri might not stumble upon the box accidentally.

The little house in the woods.

If he took the box there, he'd be getting it

out of the house as per Terri's request and placing it somewhere secure. As far as he could tell, no one went to the house that was hidden among the trees. The lack of graffiti and broken windows spoke to its isolation.

Of course, there had been signs of life there. The candle burning in the window hadn't lit itself. But Mike was sure the hand of any living person hadn't lighted it either. In fact, he was sure the candle had been burning in the window to attract him to the house because part of Jonathan Cain's life story had occurred there, most likely in the room behind the symbol-laden door.

Remember me.

Mike got his boots and laced them up tightly. As he bundled the letters and shroud back into the box, he realised that his position on ghosts had been reversed. He would once have said he was an unbeliever but he couldn't deny what he'd seen with his own eyes. So, either ghosts were real or he was going mad. It was much easier to accept the existence of the paranormal than it was to face the possibility of mental issues.

He placed the box beneath his arm and stole out through the back door into the dark night.

14

COMMUNICATION

July 29th

Jen awoke bleary-eyed. Sitting up groggily, she blinked at the clock on the bedside table. *10:05 a.m.*

She'd spent most of the night waking up from and falling into nightmares. Was it any wonder that her dreams had been filled with terrifying images of blood and magical symbols when her had had been holding that disgusting, bloody sheet in the kitchen?

Her reaction to the sheet had been one of sheer terror because something about it sparked memories in her head. They couldn't possibly be her own memories, of course, because she'd never been chained to a bed and covered with a sheet embroidered with those symbols but she was sure the images in her head were *someone's* memories.

Maybe they were the memories of Wendy or Claire Maxwell. She'd told Sam that she thought Simon Maxwell had only pretended to be insane but maybe she'd been wrong about that and he'd actually thought his wife and daughter were witches. If that was the case, he might have tried an exorcism or something.

And that sheet-thing had been part of it.

She shivered and got out of bed, dressing quickly in jeans and a T-shirt. When she opened her door to leave the room, she noticed something leaning against the wall in the hallway.

The Ouija board.

Chris had left it outside her room for her to find. Jen frowned at it. After giving her such a hard time when she'd asked to borrow it, why was her brother now simply giving it to her no questions asked? He never did anything unless he had something to gain from it, especially if it involved giving Jen something she wanted.

Leaving the board where it was, she turned to the stain-girl above her bed and asked, "What do you think I should—?" Her question trailed off into silence. The face was gone.

Jen got onto the bed and looked up at the

place where the stain had been to make doubly sure but it was definitely gone. The plaster on the ceiling was unblemished.

"What the hell?" she whispered to herself. How could a stain disappear?

She remembered imagining the face had detaching itself from the ceiling yesterday afternoon when she'd been lying on the bed. Had she seen it since then? Now that she thought about it, she was sure the stain hadn't been there last night but at the time she'd barely registered it because she'd been so tired.

There had to be a logical explanation. Maybe she'd been mistaken about the stain in the first place and just imagined it. Had it ever been there at all? It could have been nothing more than a trick of light and shadows on the plaster.

That explanation rang hollow. The girl's face had been there on the ceiling; Jen had seen it clearly.

And she'd seen it float down toward her as she lay on the bed until it had filled her vision.

What had happened after that? Had it passed through her and floated down to the ceiling below her bedroom?

Or had it somehow attached itself to her? Been absorbed into her?

She jumped up from the bed and checked

herself in the mirror on the dressing table. She looked the same. There was no visible sign that anything had happened to her, that someone else was inhabiting her body.

"Are you in there?" she asked her reflection. "Claire Maxwell, is that you?"

There was no reply, of course, and she shook her head at herself. "You're like a kid sitting in front of a mirror about to chant "Bloody Mary" three times. Get a grip, Jen."

She walked to the door and picked up the Ouija board and the planchette. There was a simple way to settle this. She'd use the board. If nothing happened, it would prove the house wasn't haunted. If something did happen, and she made contact with a spirit…well, she was just going to have to deal with that situation if it arose. She was hoping it wouldn't.

She didn't want to use the Ouija board in her bedroom in case her mum walked in in. One of the empty rooms would be better, more private.

"Right, let's do it," she told herself.

But as she was about to leave the room, a voice whispered in her mind. *The woods.*

Jen hesitated. She felt a sudden compulsion to go to the woods, despite telling herself yesterday that she was going to avoid the place.

Had that thought been her own or was something inside her trying to control her?

She shrugged it off and continued to the spare room farther along the hallway but as she put her hand on the doorknob to enter the room, the thought returned. *The woods.*

The thought was difficult to resist because it seemed like it was her own, even though she had no idea why she'd be telling herself to take the Ouija board to the woods.

She hesitated, her hand still on the doorknob of the spare room.

The woods.

"All right, the woods," she said, turning away from the door and returning to her bedroom. If she was going to go to the woods again, there were some things she was going to need to take with her.

First, she thought about wearing the phone on the armband again but that hadn't worked last time. The video had frustratingly missed just about everything because of the angle it had been worn at on her arm.

Wondering how she was going to get around that problem and unwilling to go to the woods without some kind of video record, Jen cast a glance at the MacBook sitting on her dressing table. That gave her an idea. She opened it up and tethered it to her phone. Since she was going into the woods, she'd need to use her phone's data to get a signal.

Then she opened up Face Time and called her best friend Emma.

The call connected immediately and Emma's face appeared on the screen. As soon as she saw her friend's warm brown eyes and infectious smile, Jen missed her twice as hard as before. She and Emma had been friends all through school and the only thing that kept Jen sane was the fact that, after the summer, they were both going to the London College of Fashion together.

"Hey, girlfriend," Emma said, "I was just thinking about you. What's up?"

"Emma, I need you to do me a favour. I'm going to go into the woods and use this." She held up the Ouija board so Emma could see it.

Emma's eyes widened. "A Ouija board? Girl, what are you doing? You don't even believe in any of that stuff."

"I know," Jen said. "At least I didn't. Now, I don't know what I believe. I want to take you with me while I go to the woods and use this, okay? I want you to witness what happens in case I...black out or something."

"Black out? Jen, you need to tell me what's going on. You're scaring me."

"I can't explain everything right now," Jen

said, putting the planchette into the back pocket of her jeans and picking up the board and laptop. "But I think there may be a ghost or something in the house, or in the woods, or both, I'm not sure. Some weird shit has been happening."

"Like what? Tell me everything."

"I will. But for now, just tell me you'll stick with me while I do this, okay?"

"Of course I'll stick with you. I'd do anything for you, you know that."

Jen did know that, and that was why she'd called Emma and not any of her other friends. Emma was reliable and shared a bond with Jen that had been forged over the years.

Holding the MacBook in the crook of one arm, with the Ouija board tucked under her armpit, Jen left the room and went downstairs.

"Wow," Emma said, "is that your house? It's huge."

"Yeah, it's big," Jen said. She thought of the stain on her bedroom ceiling. "And creepy."

Emma leaned closer to the camera and whispered, "So what's with the Ouija board? Who are you trying to contact?"

"There's a girl who died here in the 1970s," Jen said as she reached the hallway. "I think she's been trying to contact me." She might have felt foolish saying this to anyone else but

Emma was a believer in ghosts and once claimed to have seen her grandmother's spirit. At the time, Jen had thought her friend crazy or mistaken but had said nothing to dissuade Emma of her belief; friends didn't do that to each other. Knowing what she knew now, though, Jen wondered if Emma had seen her dead grandmother after all.

"How is she contacting you?" Emma asked.

Jen decided it would take too much time to explain the stain on the ceiling and the way it had drifted down toward her so instead, she said, "I'm not exactly sure. It's just a feeling, you know?"

Emma nodded in understanding. "It's just like when I saw my grandma. I had a feeling it was going to happen and then I saw her standing there in our living room. Have you seen this girl?"

Jen wasn't sure how to answer that. She'd seen someone in the woods, had spoken to them, but she couldn't remember anything about it and her stupid phone had only picked up static. "Maybe, I'm not exactly sure."

"How did she die?"

"Just a second, I need to be quiet," Jen whispered. She could hear the TV in the living room and assumed her mum was in there watching it. She crept past the room, anxious to get outside without having to explain to her mum why she was going to the woods and why she had a Ouija board under her arm.

She reached the kitchen and made sure the coast was clear before crossing to the back door and leaving the house. Once outside, she pushed the back gate open with her hip and made her way around the lake to the trees.

"Her name was Claire Maxwell and was murdered," she told Emma.

"Murdered? Jen, you need to be careful, girl, she might be a vengeful spirit or something like that." Emma peered at the camera. "Is that a lake behind you?"

Jen nodded. "It's right outside our back gate."

"Wow, that's amazing. Your own outdoor swimming pool."

"Yeah, maybe," Jen said. "The lake has a creepy history as well, though. It was used to drown witches back in the day."

Emma's eyes widened even further. "Okay, I just got some major chills. Are you sure it's a good idea to be playing with a spirit board in that place?"

I don't have a choice, Jen thought. *I have to know what's happening to me.* "I'll be okay," she told Emma. "You're here, right? What can go wrong?"

"A lot," Emma said seriously. "Give me a couple of seconds. I'm going to Google this Claire Maxwell chick and see if there's anything about her online." She began tapping on her keyboard.

Jen mentally kicked herself for not thinking about doing that earlier. She'd assumed that everything Sam had told her about the Maxwells had been everything there was to know. She hadn't considered researching the house herself, which was unlike her but probably understandable given the stress she'd been under lately.

"Look up Crow House," she told Emma. "That's the name of the house."

Emma looked up from her keyboard and arched an eyebrow. "Crow House? Did your dad just relocate your family into one of those Hammer horror movies or something?"

Jen nodded. "I know, right?"

"You wouldn't find me within ten miles of that place," Emma said. "At least tell me there's an upside to living there. What are the local boys like? Cute?"

Jen thought of Sam Wetherby and smiled. "Maybe."

"You've met someone!" Emma exclaimed. "Tell me all about him. What's his name?"

"I haven't met anyone, not in that way. There's a guy in the village who seems nice."

"Nice? You're going to have to expand on that. How did you meet? And what do you mean "nice?" Nice face? Nice butt?"

Jen rolled her eyes. "He's just a nice guy. He gave me a lift when I...got lost this one time. His name's Sam."

"Sam, huh?" Emma grinned. "You have to give me more than that." Then the smile vanished and she wrinkled her nose. "It says here that Claire Maxwell was murdered by her father Simon because he thought she was a witch. She was drowned in that lake along with her mother."

"I know," Jen said, "that's what Sam told me." She was in the woods now, moving through the undergrowth, looking for somewhere to place the Ouija board on the ground.

"But did you also know that another family went missing from Crow House in 1892?"

Jen shook her head.

"According to this site, the Cain family vanished on August 1st 1892. And it says here that the father, Jonathan Cain, believed his wife Mary to be a witch. They had a daughter named Elizabeth. That's all it says about the Cains. There's more info on the Maxwell family because that was more recent but don't you think it strange that both men thought their wives were witches?"

"I don't know," Jen said, spotting a small clearing that would be a good place to use the Ouija board. She walked over to it and put the board on the ground. "Maybe."

"Maybe?" Emma said. "It's obvious what happened; the ghost of Jonathan Cain possessed Simon Maxwell and history repeated itself." She frowned and then added, "Is your dad acting strangely at all?"

"No stranger than normal," Jen said, taking the planchette from her pocket.

"Do you think he could be possessed by the ghost of Jonathan Cain?"

"What? No! Don't say that."

Emma shook her head slowly. "I'm sorry, hun, but you have to face facts. If this Jonathan Cain dude possessed Simon Maxwell in the 1970s, then there's no reason why he couldn't possess your dad today."

"That's stupid," Jen said. "My dad might be weird but he isn't possessed." *In fact*, she thought to herself, remembering the stain floating down toward her from the ceiling, *I might be the one who's possessed.*

She placed the laptop against a tree and sat own in front of the Ouija board, ready to call the spirits. She'd never done this before and she had no idea what she was supposed to do. Was the planchette supposed to start in a particular place on the board?

"I'm not sure how to do this," she told Emma.

"Hang on, I'll look it up." Emma tapped in her keyboard and then said, "Okay, you have to move the planchette in a clockwise circle around the board and say, "If there are any spirits who wish to talk to me, you may do so through this board." That's called petitioning the spirits. And then you put the planchette in the centre of the board and ask a question or something."

Jen did what Emma had described, feeling more than a little foolish as she told the spirits they could use the board to talk to her. She returned the planchette to the middle of the board and tried to think of a question. "What shall I ask?" she whispered to Emma.

"Ask if there's anyone there," Emma whispered back.

Jen cleared her throat. "Is there anyone there?"

Her fingers rested lightly on the planchette. It didn't move. She looked at Emma and whispered, "Nothing's happening."

"They might be having trouble communicating. Ask another question."

"Does anyone want to talk? Hello?" Jen asked, looking down at the board.

Still nothing. The planchette felt like a dead weight beneath her fingers.

"I don't think it's working," Emma said. "Hey, I have to go in a minute, I'm meeting Sarah at Starbucks."

"Oh, okay," Jen said, disappointed not only in the failure of the Ouija board to provide her with any answers but also the fact that she was miles away from her friends. She wished she could go to Starbucks with Emma and Sarah but knew that until this summer was over, she was going to be isolated from everyone. Would they still welcome her back into the group after more time had passed? What if they didn't?

"Are you going to keep trying?" Emma asked.

Jen shook her head. "No, I don't see the point."

"Before you end a session on a Ouija board, you have to say goodbye," Emma said. "It closes the door to the spirit world or something."

"Goodbye," Jen said with a note of finality, unsure if she was talking to the spirits or Emma. Was she closing the door on the spirits or was Emma closing the door on her? She imagined Emma and Sarah at Starbucks, talking about boys, and music, and clothes, and then Emma would say, "Hey, I spoke to Jen earlier," and Sarah would say, "Cool, how was she?" and Emma would reply, "Fine," and then they'd go back to talking about boys and all that other stuff and Jen would be forgotten.

"Keep in touch," Emma said. She looked closely at Jen through the camera. "Hey, are you okay?"

Jen shrugged. "Yeah, I'm fine."

"Keep me informed about the ghosts, okay? Talk to you later." She ended the call and the screen went blank. Jen closed the MacBook. She looked at the Ouija board. She should have known Chris and his friend would make a useless piece of junk. Chris had even told her it didn't work, so why had she bothered trying to use it? She'd just made a fool of herself.

And now she felt worse than she'd ever felt since arriving at this damned house because she'd just discovered that her friends in London were getting on with their lives absolutely fine without her. It was as if she'd never existed.

She started when she thought she heard a voice among the trees, a girl's voice saying, "Hello." She turned her head in the direction the voice had come from.

And the next thing she knew she was standing on a rock that jutted out into the lake, the laptop and the Ouija board tucked under her arm. Darting her head around in panic, she saw Crow House across the lake and calmed down a little; at least she hadn't strayed too far this time but how had she arrived at this rock? What had happened since hearing the voice and waking up here?

Waking up probably wasn't the right term; she hadn't been asleep. She was standing up, not lying down. So, if not asleep, then what? Hypnotised? Sleepwalking?

She felt too afraid to stay here any longer. Something had brought her here, forced her to come here while she was blacked out. Now that she had her senses back, she need to leave.

Turning toward the trees, she resisted the urge to flee in a blind panic. She needed to remain calm if she was going to get home. Running blindly would only get her lost in the woods. As long as she kept the lake in view, she could use it to navigate her way home.

After she'd been walking for a couple of minutes, she turned to see how far she'd come from the rock.

What she saw there made her heart hammer in her chest. A dark-haired girl dressed in a white night gown stood by the rock, peering into the lake. As Jen watched, the girl began to walk forward, calmly moving deeper and deeper until she disappeared completely beneath the water.

Jen ran.

15

SUSPICION

Mike was tidying up the front garden, trying to keep his mind focused on menial tasks. Being touched by Cain's ghost had frightened him and was something he'd rather not think about. Throwing himself into gardening had seemed like a good idea but it wasn't helping him forget that ghostly touch on his forehead.

Terri seemed to have moved on from the argument, or at least she wasn't mentioning it. She was spending the day in her studio, which Mike supposed was her way of distracting herself from the fissures that were appearing in their family unit.

He heard a car on the road and looked up from the weeds he'd just attacked with the grass trimmer to see a green Range Rover trundling toward the house. The vehicle stopped next to the Sportage and DCI Battle climbed out, giving Mike a brief wave.

Mike killed the trimmer and leaned it against the wall before heading to the gate to greet the detective. He felt a slight sting of embarrassment when he remembered his last encounter with Battle but that feeling was suppressed by curiosity as to why the man was here now.

Terri came out of the house and joined Mike at the gate. "What's he doing here?" she whispered.

"I have no idea," Mike whispered back to her. Then he raised his voice and said, "Can I help you, detective?"

Battle gave them a smile. "I was in the area, so I thought I'd pay you a visit and see how you're settling in. I'm not here on official business, it's just a social call."

"I'll put the kettle on," Terri said before disappearing into the house. As she went, she shot Mike a questioning look and he offered a slight shrug by way of a reply. He thought it strange that the local Detective Chief Inspector should pay them a social call but wondered if that was the way things were done in the countryside where everyone knew everyone else's business.

"That would be lovely, Mrs Wilson," Battle

called after her, seemingly oblivious to the exchange between Terri and Mike. Turning to Mike, he said, "Are you settling in all right, sir? Now that your furniture's here, I mean."

"Yes, we're getting used to it slowly," Mike said, opening the gate to let the detective into the newly trimmed garden. "It's very different to London."

"Oh, yes, I have no doubt. I expect you find everything a bit quieter here. No noisy neighbours, eh?"

"Not unless you count the birds and squirrels," Mike said. He had the feeling the detective was here on more than just a social call, that there was something the man wanted to say but was feeling his way there slowly.

Battle chuckled. "Yes, quite." He pointed at the house. "I've been out here a few times, you know. During my career, I mean. I suppose you know about that nasty business in the 70s."

Mike shook his head. "No, what do you mean?"

"There was a tragedy here. Not in the house, exactly, but at the lake. The family lived in the house at the time, though. The Maxwells. Simon, his wife Wendy, and their daughter Claire. Simon killed both of them. Drowned them in the lake. Said they were witches."

Mike had never played poker but now he

tried to put on a poker face so as not to show his emotions. At the mention of Wendy Maxwell's husband thinking her a witch, he'd felt a sense of shock. It sounded as if history had repeated itself in Crow House, with Simon Maxwell doing exactly what Jonathan Cain had done eighty years earlier, suspecting his wife of practicing witchcraft.

An image of the last few pages in Wendy Maxwell's diary came to Mike's mind. That nonsense word scrawled over and over on the pages. Wendy hadn't necessarily been a witch but she seemed to have lost her mental faculties while living in Crow House.

"I was just a young copper at the time," Battle continued, "but I'll never forget the day we found the bodies of those poor women. Simon had called us and told us what he'd done. He had no remorse. And do you know what the worst thing was?"

"No," Mike said, shaking head. "What was that?"

"They said later that he'd done it because he'd gone mad. But I looked him in the eyes that day and I couldn't see any trace of madness there at all."

Terri came out of the house, balancing a tray of cups and saucers and a teapot in her hands. She set the tray down on top of the garden wall and asked, "How do you like your tea, Mr Battle? Do you take milk?"

"Milk and two sugars would be lovely," he said. "And please, call me Stewart. As I said, I'm not on duty. I was just telling your husband what a lovely part of the country this is. Nice and quiet. I hope you like it here."

Mike raised an eyebrow. That hadn't been what he and Battle had been discussing at all.

She screwed up her nose. "I guess I'm a city girl at heart."

"Quite understandable," Battle said. "The countryside isn't for everyone, I suppose." He took the cup of tea she offered him and took a sip. "Ah, that hits the spot. Thank you."

"If you'll excuse me," she said, "I'm in the middle of a painting."

Battle nodded. "Of course. I'll just finish my tea and then I'll be on my way. I'm sure you have a lot of work to do."

Terri smiled at him and went back into the house.

"I take it your wife doesn't like me," Battle said to Mike.

"Don't take it personally. Terri doesn't like talking about the house, this area of the country, or the reason we moved here. She misses London."

"And how about you? It seems to me that you've settled in here just fine."

Mike frowned. "Why would you say that? The last time we met, you must have thought I was crazy, seeing things that weren't there."

Battle looked him dead in the eye and said, "I don't think you're crazy at all, sir. When I was here last, I saw the look on your wife's face when you were talking about that face in the window and I felt a great pity for her. That's why I didn't mention to her what we were talking about just now. It's also why I came here to tell you to be wary of this house. It has a bad history that seems to resurface every now and then."

"You mean the Maxwells?"

"The Maxwells," Battle said, "and also the family that lived here originally. The Cains."

Mike said nothing.

"Now you probably think *I'm* crazy," Battle said light-heartedly. He studied the trees that stood near the house as he sipped his tea and then said, "But I've lived in this area all my life and over the years, I've come to believe that these woods are a bad place. We've had plenty of hikers go missing without a trace in this area. That kind of thing only happens occasionally and sometimes years go by before it happens again, so nobody connects the disappearances, but if you look at the big picture, this area is like a Bermuda Triangle and Crow House is at the centre of it."

Mike wasn't surprised to hear the detective's words. He realised the house had a bad reputation with the locals and given what he'd experienced here, he couldn't say that reputation was unwarranted. But this was the first time he'd heard of hikers going missing in the woods.

Misreading Mike's thoughtful silence as an unwillingness to talk, Battle said, "I can see I've overstepped my bounds, sir. I'll be on my way."

"No, it's fine," Mike told him. "I was just thinking about the house and its reputation. No wonder my uncle got the place cheap."

"Don't get me wrong," Battle said, "quite a few families have lived in Crow House over the years without incident. But they never stayed for long."

"Did you warn them about the house? Maybe that had something to do with them moving away."

Battle chuckled but there was little humour in it. "No, I didn't warn them. After what happened to the Maxwells, though, I try to keep an eye on this place."

Understanding dawned in Mike. "And that's

why you, and not a uniformed officer, responded to our call."

"That's right. Although DS Lyons and I actually *were* in the area at the time your call came in, so I could respond without anyone at the station asking why a detective was attending a suspected intruder case."

"And because of my behaviour during that visit, you felt the need to come back here today and warn me about the house, or the woods, or whatever it is you're warning me about. I'm not too clear on that part. Are you saying Crow House is haunted?"

Battle turned his eyes to the house and frowned. "I'm not sure what I'm saying, Mr Wilson. I can't deny that there are some strange goings-on in this area. They used to drown women who were suspected of witchcraft in that lake, you know. Hundreds of years ago, I mean. The lake was a drowning pool. That might be where Simon Maxwell got the idea to drown his wife and daughter but the question isn't where he got the inspiration for the murder method but why did he murder his family in the first place? Was he possessed by something from the past?"

"Like a ghost?" Mike asked, recalling Jonathan Cain's ghost walking across the kitchen and touching his forehead while whispering, "Remember me."

"Perhaps," Battle said. "The original occupants of the house, the Cain family, disappeared one night but apparently, Jonathan Cain had accused his wife of witchcraft in letters to his friend, a respected doctor in London. Eerily similar to Simon Maxwell, eh?"

"I suppose so," Mike said, shrugging.

Battle eyes him closely. "You don't know anything about this already?"

"No," Mike said, putting on his poker face again. "Someone in the village tried to warn me about the house and the lake but I drove away before he could say anything. I thought he was a drunk or something."

Battle nodded knowingly. "Was it an older gentleman with a moustache?"

"Yes, that's him. He was outside the chip shop on the day we moved here."

"That's Eric Maxwell. Simon Maxwell's brother. He warns everyone who comes to the house about what happened to his brother. Insists that Simon was a respected man who would never hurt his family until Crow House got its claws into him. I might wonder about connections between Simon Maxwell and Jonathan Cain but Eric takes it one step further. He draws a connection between what happened to his brother and the old tales surrounding this area; tales of witches worshipping a demon in the woods."

"So he thinks Wendy Maxwell was a witch? That she worshipped a demon?" Mike again recalled Wendy's diary and the handwriting within that devolved until it became one single word scrawled over and over. What was that word? Geth-something. What did it mean? Had Wendy been a witch after all? And if she had, what did that mean for his own family? Jen was spending a lot of time in the woods. Perhaps there was a connection he should look into.

"I'm not sure exactly what he believes," Battle said, "but he certainly thinks there's an evil presence here that dates back to the witch trials, maybe even further back in time than that."

"You know this all sounds crazy, right?" Mike asked.

"I know exactly how it sounds, sir. You probably think we're nothing more than bunch of superstitious country bumpkins up here but I wouldn't be able to live with myself if something happened to your family and I hadn't warned you about the house."

"I can assure you, I have no intention of accusing my wife and daughter of witchcraft," Mike said with a grin.

Battle nodded slowly, like a man resigned. "I shouldn't have expected you to believe me. I'll be on my way, sir." He turned to the gate and opened it. "Give my regards to your wife and thank her for the tea." He walked to the Range Rover and got in. This time, there was no cheery wave; Battle simply started the engine and drove away, looking straight ahead and not sparing Mike even a glance.

Mike downed his tea and placed the cup on the tray before making his way inside. He went through the house to the kitchen and, through the window, saw Jen sprinting toward the house from the woods. She had her laptop under one arm, along with an object Mike didn't recognise, and she appeared to be fleeing in terror.

Mike put the tray into the sink and stepped away from window. The back door opened a couple of seconds later and Jen rushed inside, colliding with him. She managed to hold onto the laptop but dropped the other item, which Mike at first thought was nothing more than a sheet of wood but then realised, as he looked closer, was a Ouija board.

"Dad, what the hell!" She bent down quickly to retrieve the board.

"Jen, what are you doing?"

"Nothing," she said, a guilty look on her

face. She tried to push past Mike but he stopped her with a firm hand on her shoulder.

"A Ouija board isn't nothing, Jen."

She pulled away from him and went into the hall, shaking her head in either anger or embarrassment as she ascended the stairs.

Jen was the last person Mike would have expected to use a Ouija board and if he hadn't seen her running into the house with his own eyes, he'd never have believed it. Yet he *had* seen it. Jen had been in the woods with a Ouija board doing God-knew-what.

For a fleeting moment, he felt a kinship with Jonathan Cain. Wasn't this the same situation Cain had found himself in, wondering what a family member was doing in the woods? In Cain's case, it had been his wife and in Mike's, his daughter, but everything else was the same.

Jen had seemingly become obsessed with the woods and now she was using a Ouija board to communicate with...what exactly? According to local legend, a demon lived out there somewhere. Also according to local legend, women had been drowned in the lake. Could their ghosts haunt the woods, just as Jonathan Cain's ghost haunted Crow House?

He turned to the window and looked out at the lake and woods. The landscape looked idyllic but what horrors lurked beneath its surface? He would probably never know for sure but there was one thing he was certain of: if something evil was out there, he wouldn't let it sink its claws into his family.

16

REMEMBER ME

THAT NIGHT, as Mike tried to sleep, his thoughts returned to the lake and the woods. Terri slept soundly next to him, oblivious to what Jen had been doing today. Mike had decided not to tell her; it would only upset her and there was no point in doing that. If the situation with Jen needed handling, then he would handle it alone. There was nothing to be gained by bringing Terri into it and complicating things further.

Resigned to the fact that he would get no sleep tonight, he slipped out of bed and padded to the window. When he looked out, he was surprised to see a full, silver moon in the night sky. That couldn't be right; when he'd seen the moon earlier, it had been no more than three-quarters full.

He turned back to the room and started when he realised it had changed. The double bed he and Terri shared, the bed he had just slipped out of was gone, replaced by a four-poster bed Mike had never seen before. Terri was also gone and the room, as were the packing boxes that had been stacked in the corner.

The room was now furnished with dark, wooden furniture ornamented with brass handles. A clock on the wall ticked steadily, its pendulum swinging with metronomic precision.

Mike shrank back against the wall, feeling disoriented and dizzy. Was he dreaming? Had he fallen asleep and was all of this happening in his head?

He didn't know what to do, hardly dared to breathe, never mind move. Willing himself to wake up, he pinched the skin on his forearm. He felt the pain but didn't wake up in his own bed, next to his wife. He remained here, in the bedroom as it had been in the past.

The door opened and Jonathan Cain walked in. He looked just as he had when Mike had seen him in the kitchen, dressed in a shirt and trousers and sporting a close-cropped reddish-brown beard. He strode over to the window and looked out at the moonlit landscape, ignoring Mike.

Gaining a little more courage now that he knew he couldn't be seen, Mike stepped closer to the window and followed the man's gaze. Far below, the back garden looked well tended and in bloom with roses and honeysuckle. A flash of white in the woods caught Mike's attention and he realised it was a woman dressed in a white nightgown running through the trees. She had long fair hair that flowed behind here as she ran and covered her face when she cast a terrified glance behind her. If someone was chasing her, Mike couldn't see who that person might be.

"Mary," Jonathan whispered before turning away from the window and striding across the room to a piece of furniture Mike recognised as the bureau that was locked in the cellar in his own time but was obviously part of the bedroom furniture in whatever-year-this-was.

Opening the top drawer, Jonathan removed a thick leather-bound book whose cover bore no title, only a gilt pentagram set into the leather. He leafed through the pages quickly and Mike saw more occult symbols on the fast-turning pages along with dense writing and illustrations of creatures he didn't recognise but which looked like they'd sprung up from the deepest pits of Hell.

Seemingly finding the page he was searching for, Jonathan seized a leather bookmark from among the clutter on the bureau and thrust it into the book before closing the tome and heading downstairs with it clutched in his hands.

Mike followed. He didn't want to be left alone in the strange bedroom and he had a feeling that Cain's ghost touching his forehead and saying, "Remember me," was somehow connected to what was unfolding before his eyes at this moment. He was sure the ghostly touch had triggered this dream vision and that something important was about to unfold that he was supposed to see.

He followed Jonathan downstairs and out through the back door into the moonlit garden. The fragrance of the roses and honeysuckle was cloyingly sweet in the warm night air.

When he reached the gate, Cain called, "Mary! Come back! Where are you?"

When no reply was forthcoming, he set off at a steady run toward the woods, Mike in tow.

They headed for the little house and when they reached it, Mike saw that it was in a much better condition than it would be when he'd stumble upon the place over a century later.

Cain groaned, "No," when he saw that the white-painted front door was wide open. He sprinted inside and bounded up the steps to the upper room. The bed was there, only now it had a grubby mattress sitting atop the metal frame. The open shackles attached to the corners of the frame were covered with fresh blood.

After searching his trouser pockets, Cain whispered, "She took the key. Eliza took the key." He went back downstairs and out through the front door to the trees, where he called Mary's name again. There was still no answer but now Mike noticed—as did Cain—a figure in white running toward the house. Unlike Mary, though, this girl had dark hair.

"Eliza," Cain shouted, setting off after his daughter. "What have you done? Why have you released her?"

Ignoring him, the girl fled into the house.

Cain increased his pace, stopping only when he got to the gate. As Mike stood next to the bearded man, he could see that Cain's reason for pausing was not only to regain his breath but also to compose himself. There were tears in his eyes and his rapid breath hitched in his throat.

He sagged against the gatepost and for a moment, Mike thought the man was going to collapse. But Jonathan Cain pushed himself upright and seemed to steel himself. He strode through the back garden and into the house.

"Eliza," he called as he entered the house. "Where are you?"

Eliza didn't reply but Mike thought he could hear her crying somewhere in the house. Cain seemed to hear it too, cocking his head to listen more closely. Both men realised at the same moment that the sound was coming from the cellar.

"Eliza," Cain said, striding toward the cellar door. "What are you doing down there? Why did you unshackle your mother?"

The crying abated for a moment and the girls' voice came floating up the stairs. "I don't know, Father. It made me do it." Then she began to sob.

Cain descended the stairs to the dirt floor of the cellar and Mike followed. A lantern hung from the ceiling where, in Mike's time, there would be a dim bulb. The lantern cast a circle of light over the cellar floor and Mike could see the girl huddled in the corner of the room, her face hidden by her dark hair, her body hitching as she sobbed.

"Eliza," Cain said, his tone softening, "what has happened to you?"

Between gasps for breath, the girl said, "I... didn't want to...Father. It made me."

Cain crouched down before her and put a hand on her shoulder. "Come now, child. Who made you? What are you talking about?"

Eliza stopped crying and whispered, "He who roams the woods."

Cain got to his feet and took a few steps back from his daughter. "Eliza, has your mother infected you with her witchcraft? I told you to stay away from her. I told you to ignore her evil ramblings and now you say these words that could have come from her own wicked mouth."

The girl began to cry again. "I'm sorry. It made me do it. I couldn't resist. I released her and then I came down here, just like it told me."

Cain's eyes darted to the shadows in the cellar, a panic entering his voice. "It told you to come down here? Why?"

"I don't know," she bawled, shaking her head, her face still hidden by her hair and the darkness.

"Eliza, look at me," Cain told her. "Why did it tell you to come down here?"

Slowly, the girl turned her face toward her father. Mike could see a family resemblance between the two, even though half of Eliza's face was hidden by her hair. Then he noticed blood running down her neck and staining the white nightgown.

Cain must have noticed it too because he said, "Eliza, what's happened to you?"

In answer, the girl swept the hair away from her face.

Mike started. A pentagram had been carved into her flesh. It reached all the way to her forehead at its uppermost point. The lower points of the symbol terminated on Eliza's cheek so that her eye was at its centre.

"Eliza!" Cain shouted, shocked.

"It made me do it," she said. "It made me do it." Tears flowed from her eyes, catching the light from the lantern as they rolled down her cheeks.

Mike felt a deep rumbling beneath his feet. He looked down at the dirt floor, wondering if he was experiencing an earthquake. The tremor rose intensity until the whole house seemed to be shuddering around them. The lantern swung wildly, throwing a chaotic pattern of shadows over the cellar walls.

The floor suddenly exploded beneath their feet, throwing up a fountain of earth that hit the ceiling and rained down over everything, leaving a grave-sized hole in the centre of the room.

Eliza's eyes were wide with fear. "It's here,"

she whispered, scrabbling back into the corner of the room.

Cain cried out and Mike turned to the man in time to see him being thrown through the air and into the hole in the dirt floor. Cain landed on his back, his arms clutching the book to his chest.

"Father!" Eliza cried.

"Eliza, run!" Cain shouted at her. "Get out of this house!"

The girl shook her head. "No, I can't leave you here."

"Go!" he shouted.

Sobbing, the girl got to her feet and fled the room, scrambling up the cellar steps.

At that moment, Jonathan Cain turned his eyes toward Mike, looking directly at him.

Mike wondered if Jonathan had been aware of his presence the entire time and was only now acknowledging it.

"Remember me," Cain said to Mike.

Then the earth that had erupted from the hole rushed back into it, burying Jonathan Cain alive.

And Mike woke up with a start, bathed in sweat. He sat up and looked around the dark room, disoriented at first but then gradually becoming aware that he was in bed with Terri sleeping beside him and that the nightmare had been just that: a nightmare.

Terri stirred and mumbled, "Are you okay?"

"I'm fine," he said, looking out at the night sky where the moon was again three-quarters full. "Go back to sleep."

That was something he was sure he wouldn't be able to do himself so he slipped out of bed and went downstairs to the living room. Once there, he kept the lights off and sat in his armchair in the dark.

Why did Cain put that dream, vision...or whatever the hell it was...into my head?

He replayed the dream in his head, from the moment he'd appeared in the bedroom to the moment Jonathan Cain had said, "Remember me" as he was being buried alive.

He's still down there, Mike thought. *Buried beneath the cellar. He's been there all this time.*

Then, another thought came to him. *And so has the book.*

Was Cain trying to let me know that the book is in the cellar? He remembered Cain grabbing the book and thrusting a bookmark into a specific page. Something on that page must have been important and Cain was showing him where the book was.

All Mike had to do was dig up the cellar and find the book, which was clutched in Cain's dead hands.

"I can do this," he muttered. But then he wondered if he *should* do it. Why not just move to another house? The sensible thing to do would be to pack up their belongings and put Crow House in their rearview mirror.

"We can't leave," he whispered to himself, feeling the sting of embarrassment at losing his job. "This house is our last chance to get back on our feet."

Also, he wasn't sure if the evil here had already changed Jen in some way. She spent a lot of time in the woods. She'd even been out there with a Ouija board.

Had the evil already infected her?

If it had, then Mike had no choice; he had to destroy the evil being that roamed among the trees.

17

RESOLVE

July 30th

The next day, Mike discovered that he'd have to drive all he way to Matlock to reach the nearest hardware store.

He needed to obtain a spade to dig up the cellar floor so he'd told Terri earlier that he was going to the shops and had jumped into the Sportage before checking the location of the nearest store on his phone. As he'd been doing that, Chris had come out to the car and asked if he could come too. Unable to think of any reason why his son shouldn't accompany him, Mike had told Chris to jump in.

The nearest store had turned out to be in Matlock, the closest large town to Shawby. The

SatNav had directed them there and now, as Mike pulled into the car park that served half a dozen shops, including a coffee house, furnishing store, and the hardware store, he realised that he felt a sense of relief at being away from Crow House.

He parked the Sportage and climbed out, taking a moment to reassess his recent decision to fight the evil in the woods. Standing here beneath the warm summer morning sun, miles away from the problems at Crow House, he could hardly believe the recent events involving ghosts and time-travelling dreams had actually happened. Did he really think a demon prowled the woods only twenty miles away from where he now stood? Was it possible?

"I don't know," he told himself, locking the car.

"What did you say?" Chris asked, coming around the side of the car with his phone in hand.

"Just talking to myself," Mike told him. "Nothing important."

Chris grinned. "Talking to yourself must run in our family."

"What do you mean by that?"

"Nothing," Chris said, chuckling to himself.

Mike frowned at his son, certain that the

boy was up to something. "Come on, Chris, spill."

Chris seemed to think about that and then sighed. "All right, but you have to promise not to get mad or anything."

Mike arched an eyebrow. "How can I promise that if I don't know what you're going to tell me?"

Chris went silent.

"Chris, tell me."

"All right, all right." Chris threw his arms up in mock surrender. "So, a couple of days ago, Jen came to me wanting to borrow my Ouija board."

"What?" Mike said, shocked. "I didn't even know you had a Ouija board."

"It's no big deal, Dad. Scott Jones and I made it a couple of years ago. Anyway, that isn't the point. The point is, Jen wanted to borrow it."

"Why?"

"That's the question I asked myself. I mean, Jen isn't exactly the type of person who believes in ghosts, am I right? Anyway, we had a bit of a disagreement and she stormed out of my room. So I got to thinking—"

"Chris, get to the point."

"Right. So anyway, as you know I have a popular YouTube channel."

Mike didn't know that at all, at least not the

popular part. He knew Chris dicked about on the Internet looking at videos of ghosts and Bigfoot but he didn't know Chris had his own channel.

"So I decided that a video of my skeptical sister using a Ouija board would be interesting to my viewers," Chris said. "So I put the board outside Jen's room. That way, she could borrow it without having to go through the embarrassment of asking me. She was clearly embarrassed so I was saving her from being uncomfortable."

"You're all heart," Mike said. "I don't suppose this had anything to do with you wanting to post a video of her online."

Chris shrugged. "Regardless of my motives, what you'll really be interested in is what happened next."

"I'm all ears," Mike said.

"So Jen came out of her room and found the board," Chris said, tapping on his phone. "She took it into the woods and I followed her."

"I thought you were scared of the woods."

Chris grimaced. "Yeah, they're pretty spooky but I was willing to follow Jen in there because I was sure I'd get some footage that would be pure gold. And I wasn't wrong. Dad, you have to see this." He passed the phone to Mike and said, "Press play."

Mike looked at the screen, which showed a static image of Jen in the woods. The Ouija board was on the ground in front of her, along with her open laptop. Mike hit play and the video started.

Jen was talking to the laptop. "Yeah, I'm fine."

"Who is she talking to?" Mike asked Chris.

"Her friend Emma. Just keep watching."

A voice came out of the laptop, tinny and difficult to hear on Chris's video. "Keep me informed about the ghosts, okay? Talk to you later."

Jen leaned forward and closed the laptop. She sat silently for a moment, as if in contemplation, and then looked up as if she'd seen someone approaching or heard something out of the ordinary. She got to her feet and said, "Hello."

Mike peered closer at the phone, trying to see who his daughter was talking to.

"You won't see anyone, Dad," Chris said. "I was right there and I can assure you that there was no one else around. Jen was talking to herself. Crazy, right?"

Ignoring him, Mike watched Jen on the screen. She said, "I was trying to contact—" and stopped as if someone had interrupted her.

"Are you sure there was no one else there?"

Mike asked Chris. "If you were hiding, you might not have been able to see them from your vantage point."

"Dad, I'm telling you, there was no one there. The only people in the woods were Jen and me."

On the screen, Jen spoke again. "Eliza. That's a pretty name."

Mike felt a finger if ice creep along the back of his neck. His daughter was speaking to the ghost of Eliza Cain. What was wrong with Jen? How could she be so calm?

"Watch this next bit closely," Chris said, chuckling. "It proves Jen is totally nuts."

Jen held out her hand and shook it as if she were shaking hands with an invisible person.

"Crazy right?" Chris asked.

Mike could see why Chris would think that. He'd have thought it himself if he'd seen this video a few days ago but now he only felt a sense of fear that crept slowly up the back of his neck.

"What are you doing out here?" Jen asked her invisible companion.

"What do you think, Dad?' Chris asked. "Do we need to commit Jen to a mental hospital or what? I mean that, right there, is all the evidence you'd need to have her locked away in a padded cell." When Mike didn't respond, he added, "Of course, you might not want to do that. Her being your daughter and all."

"Sssh," Mike said. He'd missed some of the one-sided conversation on the video.

The next words Jen spoke made Mike's blood run cold. "He who roams the woods."

That was all the conformation Mike needed. He'd heard those words in his dream vision and now his daughter had spoken them. She was somehow in contact with the spirit of Eliza Cain.

"The sisters?" Jen said on the video. After listening to whatever Eliza Cain was telling her for a couple of seconds, Jen said, "You mean the witches. The ones who were drowned in the lake." After that, Jen picked up the Ouija board and laptop and began walking away, in the direction of the lake.

"That's all I have," Chris said, holding out his hand to take the phone back. "She had a good look around before she left and I thought I should quit while I was ahead so I crept back to the house."

Mike handed over the phone. "You haven't shown this to anyone else, have you?"

Chris looked guilty. "Remember you promised not to get mad?"

"Don't tell me you posted this online."

Chris shrugged. "Maybe I did."

Mike didn't know what to say to that. He let out a long, slow breath. Chris might think this was all a joke but the video had disturbed him more than anything that had happened so far. Last night, he'd feared that Jen might be somehow infected by the evil in the woods. Now, he knew for sure that she was in contact with Eliza Cain. He recalled the pentagram carved into Eliza's face, the girl saying, "He made me do it." Eliza had been under the control of the demon and now she was talking to Jen.

The infection was real.

And the only way to deal with infection was to cut it out.

"You okay, Dad?" Chris asked, concerned.

Mike had caught sight of his reflection in the Sportage's driver's side window. He looked stressed. It showed in his eyes, in his face. Terri had probably noticed it too, probably thought it was stress over losing his job. But Mike realised he was in danger of losing something much more important than that; he could lose his entire family.

His resolve to destroy the evil became even more strengthened. He put a hand on Chris's shoulder and said, "Yeah, I'm fine. Now let's go find a spade. I need to do some digging."

They found the hardware store and went

inside. Mike went straight for the garden tools, resisting the allure of the shiny new toolboxes on the shelves. He wouldn't call himself a handyman or even an enthusiast but, like most men, he liked the idea of owning a large arsenal of tools that would allow him to leap into action whenever something needed fixing or replacing.

When he got to the garden tools section, he found for the largest spade the store carried and hefted it in his hands.

"Dad," Chris said, pulling on his arm, "look over there."

Mike followed his son's gaze and saw the old man from outside the chip shop browsing in the paint aisle. "Eric Maxwell," Mike said to himself.

"You know his name?' Chris asked.

"Yeah, the police detective was telling me about him. Eric's brother lived in Crow House a long time ago."

"Is that why he tried to warn us about the house? Does he know something we don't?"

That was exactly what Mike wanted to find out. Eric Maxwell had probably done all the research that could be done on Crow House. He might know something that would help Mike destroy the demon in the woods.

But Mike wasn't sure he wanted Chris to

become involved in any of this. His son was impressionable and hearing what Eric Maxwell had to say could scar him for life. "Chris, why don't you go wait in the car? I'll be out in a minute."

"No way. If you're going to confront that guy, I want to be here with you."

"I'm not going to confront him, I just want to speak to him."

Chris shrugged. "I still want to stay here with you."

The boy was too old to be ordered around so Mike nodded. "Okay, but remember, the guy is a bit unhinged. We can't believe anything he says."

"So why do you want to talk to him?"

"I'm just curious to know what he was trying to warn us about."

"Probably the witches Jonathan Cain mentioned in those old letters."

"Maybe," Mike said.

He paid for the spade and they took it back to the car, where they waited for Eric Maxwell to emerge from the store. Standing in the bright sun by the Sportage, Mike again found it hard to comprehend that he was about to have a serious conversation with someone about witches and demons.

When Eric Maxwell came out of the store

five minutes later, he was carrying a tin of paint and some brushes. He went over to an old Land Rover and placed his purchases in the boot before climbing into the vehicle.

Mike strode across the car park and knocked on the Land Rover's window just as the engine started. "I'm Mike Wilson," he told Maxwell through the window. "We spoke before. Briefly."

Maxwell looked at him and recognition dawned in the old man's eyes. He killed the engine and opened the car door. "Had second thoughts, have you? You want to hear what I've got to say now?"

Mike nodded slowly. "If you don't mind."

Maxwell pointed at the coffee house next to the hardware. "Buy me a coffee and we'll talk."

"Sure," Mike said.

Climbing out of the Land Rover, Maxwell looked at Chris and said, "I'm sorry if I scared you the other night, young man."

"You didn't," Chris said. Mike knew his son was lying but he respected the boy's bravado.

"Well that's all right, then," Maxwell said.

They made their way across the car park to the coffee house and when they got inside, the old man said he wanted a black coffee and sat at a table near the window.

There was a pleasant smell of bitter coffee in

the air and the place was busy, the chatter from the customers a low drone. Mike and Chris ordered the black coffee along with their own drinks—an Americano for Mike and iced frappe for Chris—and while they were waiting for the barista to make them, Chris said, "Dad, do you think the woods near our house are haunted?"

Yes, I do, Mike thought. *I believe a demon lives there and probably a load of ghostly witches too.* "No, of course not," he said.

"It's just that I keep thinking, what if Jen wasn't talking to herself after she used my Ouija board? What if she conjured something up and only she could see it?"

"I'm sure that isn't what happened, Chris. Your sister—" he paused, not sure where he was going with this. "She's a bit…disturbed by the woods. She probably thought she was talking to someone but it was just a figment of her imagination." That wasn't what he believed at all but it was better that Chris believed that.

"Okay," Chris said, sounding unconvinced.

Their drinks arrived and they took them to the table by the window where Eric Maxwell waited.

"Thank you," the old man said when Mike slid the black coffee across the table to him. After taking a sip, Maxwell looked into Mike's eyes. "What's happened to change your mind about talking to me? What have you seen?"

"It doesn't matter why I've changed my mind," Mike said, unwilling to tell Maxwell about the ghost of Jonathan Cain while Chris was sitting next to him. "I'm only interested in what you know about the house."

"Crow House," Maxwell said. "Let's call it by its proper name. Crow's scavenge on the carcasses of dead animals and that house picks apart the lives of decent folk and consumes them."

"What do you mean by that?" Chris asked, eyes wide.

"Chris, let the man speak," Mike said.

Maxwell grinned humourlessly and stared at Chris. "I'll tell you what I mean by that, young man. Everyone who lives in that house for any length of time has their life torn apart by it. It's happened in the past and it'll happen again, you mark my words."

"You mean Jonathan Cain," Chris said. "In the past, I mean. Jonathan Cain accused his wife of witchcraft."

"You've read the letters?" Maxwell asked Chris.

"No, he hasn't," Mike told him. "I have."

Turning his attention back to Mike,

Maxwell narrowed his eyes. "What about Cain's journal? Have you read that?"

"No."

"It's a leather-bound book. You'll find it in the same box as the letters. I thought you might have read it because I can see you're wearing the talisman that's mentioned in it." He pointed at Mike's chest.

Mike looked down at the outline of the talisman visible through his Black Sabbath T-shirt.

"The talisman is supposed to work in conjunction with a book called the *Daemones Mortum*," Maxwell said. "The *Daemones Mortum* is an English translation of an old book that contains spells for banishing demons. According to Jonathan Cain's journal, he managed to find a copy of it but nobody knows where it is now. The damned thing disappeared."

Mike simply nodded and took a sip of his coffee. He knew exactly where the *Daemones Mortum* was; Jonathan Cain had literally taken the book to his grave.

"Tell me how it works," he said to Maxwell.

Maxwell shrugged. "I have no idea. As I said, I haven't seen the book. According to Cain's journal, the forces unleashed by the book are so powerful that anyone who speaks the banishments must wear that talisman for protection or they'll be destroyed. Not just killed, Mr Wilson. Destroyed." He took a sip of coffee and stared out of the window at the car park. "If only Cain had used the book to banish that demon, my brother and his family would be alive today."

"So there really is a demon near our house?" Chris asked, his eyes wide in a mixture of fear and excitement.

Mike winced inwardly. Chris's enthusiasm had already made the situation worse when he'd given Jen the Ouija board. What Mike needed now—if he was going to save his family—was for his son to stay cool and have a clear head.

"Yes, there's a demon," Maxwell said, leaning toward Chris. "It's pure evil. It ruins families, tears them apart. My brother was a happily married, contented man until he moved to Crow House. Wendy and Claire were the apples of his eye and he'd never dream of harming either of them."

"Are you saying he didn't kill them?" Mike asked.

Maxwell looked at him with sad eyes. "No, I'm not saying that. Simon killed them, there's no doubt about that. He told me he'd done it when I visited him in prison, right before he committed suicide in his cell. He said he did it because of what they'd become."

He took a sip of his coffee before continuing. "He believed Wendy and Claire were somehow tainted with evil. He said that if he hadn't stopped them, they would have killed him and then made their way to the village. He was containing the evil, stopping it before it spread."

"That's like a movie I saw," Chris said excitedly. "There's a bunch of scientists at a station in the Antarctic and there's an alien that can change it's shape and—"

"Chris, this isn't a movie," Mike said.

"Okay, I was just saying."

"Well don't."

Chris took a sip of his frappe and stared out of the window sullenly.

"Since the events of 1972, I've done a lot of research," Maxwell said. "I think Simon got it wrong. I think the demon wanted him to kill those poor women as a kind of sacrifice." He lowered his voice. "It seems that long ago, there was a legend in this area of a demon that demanded a sacrifice on the Gule of August."

"Ghoul?" Mike asked.

Maxwell spelled the word. "The first day of August. Lammas Day, as it's called now. A long time ago, a sacrifice was taken to the woods on the Gule of August and left there for the demon. Times have changed, of course, and women aren't left in the woods as sacrifices anymore so I think the demon has become resourceful over the years and found a way to take what it needs."

"The missing hikers," Mike mused, remembering what Battle had told him.

Maxwell nodded. "The missing hikers. Two or three go missing every year but at least one of them goes missing on the first of August. I went to the police with my theory but they thought I was a crackpot. They thought I was suggesting there was a serial killer who struck once a year, a Lammas Day Murderer, if you will. I told them I was suggesting something much worse than that and they laughed me out of the station. They thought I'd gone crazy like Simon, or that I was clutching at straws to prove his innocence."

He looked pointedly at Mike. "No one should live in that house. I tried to buy it in 1972 just to stop anyone else from owning it but I couldn't afford it and the bank ended up repossessing it." He chuckled mirthlessly. "Since then, it's had a handful of owners but they never stayed there long before moving away. I suggest you do the same, Mr Wilson."

"We don't have a choice," Mike told him.

"The house is all we have right now, we don't have any option but to live there."

"No," Maxwell said. "Your family is all you have and if you don't get out of Crow House, you'll lose them." He finished his coffee and banged the cup down onto the saucer. "I suppose you're just as stubborn as that relative of yours, the one who bought the house. I told him what had happened there in the past, tried to tell him more, but he was having none of it. Couldn't wait to buy the place." He pushed his chair back and got up. "Well now I've tried to warn you as well so whatever happens next isn't my responsibility."

"Wait," Mike said, getting up and grabbing Maxwell by the arm. "What do you mean you tried to warn my relative? Uncle Rob has never been here. He bought the house sight unseen."

Maxwell raised an eyebrow. "Is that what he told you? He's been here all right. He lived in the house for two weeks after he bought it. I don't know if something scared him away or if he just had other places to be but after those two weeks, he left."

He chuckled. "For your sake, I hope he just had somewhere else to be. Because it doesn't say much for your relationship with him if he was scared away from Crow House and then he let you move in, does it?"

Mike remembered Rob suggesting that Mike and his family move into Crow House. And he was sure that Rob had also suggested they move on July 25th, the same date the Maxwells had arrived at the house. Did Rob know more about the place than he'd let on? Why had he lied to Mike and said he'd never been there?

"Take my advice," Eric Maxwell said, "and leave that house as soon as you can. Go somewhere else, anywhere else, and never look back. There's only one day left before the Gule of August. Use that time to pack up and go." He shrugged free of Mike's grip and left the coffee house.

"Dad," Chris said, "what the hell is going on?"

Watching the old man cross the car park and climb into his Land Rover, Mike said nothing while he attempted to process the information he'd gleaned. Uncle Rob had lived in the house but had blatantly lied to Mike about it. Why?

"Dad?" Chris repeated. "What's happening?"

"I don't know, Chris," Mike said truthfully, sitting down next to his son. "I really don't know."

18

THE OFFER

Jen stood in the back garden of Crow House, her eyes drawn to the shadowy woods. Despite telling herself she was going to stay in the house today and try to forget about the woods, she'd found herself compelled to leave her room and come out here into the garden. And now that she was here, she felt a further compulsion to open the gate and walk into the cool shadows beneath the branches.

She was sure that when the face had detached itself from the ceiling and floated down toward her, it had somehow gotten inside her head and was controlling her actions in some way. Perhaps even controlling her mind.

But even though she understood that she might be being manipulated by something inside her that didn't belong there, she couldn't resist the urge to enter the woods. She felt like an addict whose drug of choice was so close and tantalising. She wanted—needed—to be among the trees. She felt as if they were calling her with a siren song impossible to resist.

She was suddenly aware that she was opening the gate and stepping through it. She hadn't even made a conscious decision to do that yet here she was, turning towards the woods and putting one foot in front of the other as if the action of walking was as involuntary as breathing. It was something that had to be done and her body could handle it just fine without her conscious input. Jen was just along for the ride.

The shadows of the trees seemed to reach out to her like dark fingers, drawing her closer. Ahead, she saw a patch of white in the gloom and squinted against the sun to see it more clearly. Was that a girl standing beneath the trees, waiting for her? It was hard to tell because of the gloom in the woods but Jen was sure the girl's hair covered one side of her face. Her one visible eye reminded Jen of the eye in the stain on the bedroom ceiling.

I don't want to go into the woods, Jen told herself, feeling panic rise within her. *I don't want to see that girl*. But no matter how much she tried to herself that, her actions said otherwise. Her feet took her ever closer to the girl and the trees.

"Hey, Jen!"

The shout came from behind her. She willed herself to turn around so she could see who'd called her name but she couldn't do it. She was being drawn inexorably to the woods and there was nothing she could do to stop it.

"Jen!" She heard footsteps now as someone rushed along the lake's edge to catch up with her. Then she felt a hand on her shoulder and the spell that had been pulling her to the woods was broken. She felt in control of her own body again. She turned to face the person who'd saved her.

Sam Wetherby stood before her, with a look that was a mix of confusion and light-heartedness on his face. He was wearing jeans, boots, and a Pink Floyd T-shirt beneath a black leather jacket. His long hair was ruffled, as if he hadn't taken much time combing it this morning, but Jen found that cute rather than off-putting. "Didn't you hear me calling?" he asked.

"Sorry," she said, "I was miles away."

"Yeah, I saw that."

"Why are you here?" she asked. "Wait, don't tell me. You came to talk about music with my dad, right? You share the same taste." She pointed at the Pink Floyd T-shirt.

He frowned and looked down at the T-shirt. "What? No. I came to see you. I parked my bike a mile away to avoid your parents. Your mum wasn't too pleased to see me last time I was here."

"You came on a bike?"

"Yeah, my motorbike. She's my pet project. I take her out every now and then."

If he'd been wearing a helmet, that explained the ruffled hair. "She? Does she have a name?"

He blushed and shrugged. "Nah, but she's my baby, you know?"

"I see. So if you were trying to avoid my parents, were you going to knock on the front door and hide in the bushes in case one of them answered it?"

Sam shook his head. "I was going to throw stones at your bedroom window to get your attention."

"How do you know which room is mine?"

"Well, I don't," he said, looking uncomfortable. "But you did mention that it looks out over the lake so it has to be at the back of the house."

Jen laughed. "You're lucky you didn't throw a stone at the room my mum uses as a studio.

That's at the back of the house too and she's in there working at the moment."

"Well it's a good thing I saw you out here then." He gestured to the woods. "Going for a walk?"

Jen remembered the girl standing beneath the trees and jerked her head in that direction. There was nothing there but impenetrable shadow. "No, I've changed my mind," she said, shivering slightly.

"Hey, are you cold?" He took off his jacket and draped it around her shoulders.

Jen, who wasn't cold at all but appreciated the gesture, said, "Thanks" and pulled the jacket snug over her shoulders. It smelled pleasantly of leather and a light, citrus-scented aftershave.

"So, shall we go for a walk in the woods or have you still changed your mind?" he asked.

"I'd like to see your bike," she said.

"Sure. The quickest way back to the road is through the woods." He gestured toward the trees.

"I'd rather walk along the road," she told him.

He nodded. "Of course."

They cut through the garden and around the side of Crow House to get to the road before following it in the direction of the village.

"You said it's a mile away?" Jen asked.

He grinned. "Well, I may have exaggerated. It's just up ahead." He pointed to a motorcycle parked by the side of the road.

"Do you exaggerate often?' she asked him, disappointed that the bike wasn't farther away, necessitating more of a walk. She felt comfortable with Sam and after her bad experience earlier, she also felt a degree of safety in his proximity. He had saved her from walking uncontrollably into the woods, toward that girl, and Jen wasn't sure if the urge to re-enter the woods would return when Sam was gone. Despite how warm she felt beneath his jacket, she shivered again.

He looked at her, concerned. "Are you okay? You're shivering."

"I'm fine. It's just the woods. They give me the creeps."

Sam sighed. "I'm sorry about that, it's probably my fault. I didn't know Nancy was going to blurt out all that stuff about the witches. And then I got carried away and told you all that stuff about the Maxwell family. I probably should have been a bit more tactful, with you living in the house and everything."

"Don't worry about it," she told him. "It isn't your fault, or Nancy's. Is that why you came here? To apologise?"

She hoped he'd answer that he'd come here because he wanted to see her again but what he actually said caught her off-guard.

"I came here to warn you," he said.

"Warn me? About what?"

He hesitated, as if unsure how to say whatever was on his mind. Finally, he said, "The people in the village don't like outsiders making fun of the area or bringing attention to it."

Jen frowned. What was he talking about? "Okay. And you came here to tell me this why?"

"Because of the video you posted on the Internet. Look, I'm not mad at you or anything. I'm just warning you that a lot of people around here won't like it. You might want to take it down."

Now she was really confused. "Take what down? What video?"

They'd reached his bike now, a black Norton with gold trim on the petrol tank. The helmet that hung from the handlebars was also black, with two gold stripes over its crown to match the colour of the bike. The Norton gleamed in the bright sunlight, and it was clear that this machine was indeed Sam's baby.

Taking his phone from his pocket, he held it in front of her and pressed play on a video that showed Jen in the woods with the Ouija board, talking to Emma on her laptop and then seemingly talking to herself about witches and mentioning the name Eliza.

Jen couldn't believe what she was seeing. She had no memory of any of this happening. Her memories only went as far as her talking to Emma and then there was a hazy void up until the moment she'd regained her senses on the rock by the lake. This video showed that she'd either had some sort of episode where she'd lost her mind or she'd been talking to a spirit.

The video ended and Jen stared at the phone in disbelief. Who had filmed her in the woods? It had to be Chris. He'd left the Ouija board outside her door so he could follow her and film her while she used it. Why the hell had he posted this online?

She felt suddenly helpless. Not because Chris had posted the video but because she couldn't remember the time period it showed. She was doing things she had no awareness of and she was also doing things that she was aware of but had no power to stop, like when she'd been walking towards the woods earlier. She was losing control.

Hot tears pooled in her eyes and she felt her legs go weak.

"Hey," Sam said as Jen stumbled forward. "Here, lean on me." He put his arms around her and she held him tightly, pressing her face into his chest as she wept.

"It's okay," he said, stroking her back lightly, "I get that it's just a joke."

"No, it isn't," she told him through the tears. "I don't remember any of it. I remember going into the woods with the Ouija board but I don't remember talking to anyone. What's happening to me?"

He held her at arm's length and studied her face. "Are you being serious?"

Jen nodded. "It's all a blank. The same thing happened the other day when I went into the woods. That's when you found me near the village. I don't know how I got there except that I was running from something. This isn't a joke. I'm telling the truth."

"I believe you," he said, pulling her to him again.

Jen felt comfort in his arms for a few moments but then pushed away from him gently. "It's all real. The witches, the ghosts. I mentioned the name Eliza on the video. There was a family that lived here in Victorian times called the Cains and they had a daughter named Elizabeth."

Sam turned to the woods and stood with his hands on his hips, silent for a few moments before saying, "I don't know, Jen. Sure, some bad things have happened around here, and there are legends and stories, but do you really believe in ghosts?"

Jen knew that in the past, if she'd been asked such a question by a boy she liked, she'd have diluted her answer so she wouldn't appear crazy but she was beyond that now; something terrible was happening to her and the time for pretense was gone. "I believe," she told Sam. "I haven't believed in ghosts my whole life but I can't deny what's happening to me."

He turned to her and she saw what looked like pity in his eyes. "Don't you think that maybe you had all these ghost stories in your head and then you had an episode or something?"

She frowned at him. "An episode? What do you mean by that?"

He shrugged, looking uncomfortable. "You've probably been under a lot of stress lately and maybe that caused you to have a mental break."

"I'm not crazy," she told him vehemently. But even a she said the words, a niggling doubt entered her thoughts. What if she was losing her mind? She had reason to believe external forces—the stain on her bedroom ceiling and the girl she'd seen when she'd been inexorably pulled toward the woods—were influencing her. But nobody else had seen those things. They could have been a product of her imagination.

"I'm not saying you're crazy. I just mean that maybe the stress you're under—"

"Stop trying to psychoanalyze me, Sam."

He held up his hands in surrender. "Okay, I was only trying to help."

"By saying I've gone mad?"

"No, I'm not saying that. I..." he trailed off, obviously thinking better of what he'd been going to say next. "Okay, let's assume you're right and there are ghosts in the woods. What do you think they want? Why are they haunting you?"

"I don't know," she said, running through the events that had transpired since she'd been living in Crow House. "There's a house in the woods and there was a candle in the window that drew me to it. Maybe they want me to go in there for some reason."

"A house in the woods?"

Jen nodded. "It's a little house that's mostly dilapidated. But there was a lit candle in the window. When I walked away from the house, the candle was extinguished."

"Did you go inside?"

She shook her head.

"Shall we go and check it out?" he offered.

"No way, I'm not going into the woods again."

"So tell me where it is and I'll check it out."

"Why would you do that?"

He grinned. "Because I want to help you. If whatever is happening to you is connected to that house, somebody should take a look at what's inside."

"You said you don't believe in ghosts. You think I'm crazy."

He shook his head. "I didn't say that. I can see something's troubling you and I want to help, whatever it is."

She looked at him closely. "Why?"

"Because I like you, Jen. I don't like seeing you upset. If checking out this house in the woods will make you happy, then I'm up for it."

Jen didn't know what to say. She wasn't sure that Sam exploring the house would make her happy but at least it would alleviate the mystery surrounding the place.

"All right," she said. "If you're sure."

"I'm sure," he said lightly.

"But how do I know you'll be okay?"

"I've been in these woods plenty of time and I haven't been harmed yet."

"You think I'm imagining things," she said, realising that his bravado didn't come from a desire to help her but from his disbelief that there was anything harmful in the woods. "Just forget it," she told him.

"No, seriously, I'll check it out."

"It doesn't matter," she said, turning back towards Crow House. She should have known better than to tell a virtual stranger about her recent experiences. Maybe she would message Emma later and tell her what had happened.

But then she remembered that Emma was busy living her life in London and the close relationship she and Jen had once had was dead.

"Jen!" Sam called after her.

"Leave me alone," she told him. "I'll sort this out myself."

She didn't turn around until she reached the front door of the house and then, looking back along the road, she saw him standing by his bike, watching her. He gave her a slight wave.

Ignoring him, Jen opened the door and entered Crow House.

19

DIG

MIKE WAITED until everyone had gone to bed before going down to the cellar. When Terri had asked him if he was coming to bed at 11:00, he'd told her he wanted to stay up for a while. She hadn't questioned him or tried to change his mind. She'd simply gone upstairs wordlessly.

It was after midnight now and as Mike descended the cellar steps, he knew he'd been procrastinating about the task ahead. If he were simply going to dig up a buried book, that was one thing, but unearthing the remains of Jonathan Cain was something else entirely.

He flicked the switch on the wall and the bulb slowly bloomed into life, throwing its dim light over the room. Mike picked up the spade from where he'd leaned it against the wall earlier and cast his eyes over the dirt floor. He had no trouble locating the area where Cain had been buried alive after uttering the words, "Remember me."

Taking a deep breath and attempting to steel himself, he thrust the spade's blade into the floor. It barely penetrated half an inch. The dirt floor was hard-packed from a century of feet walking over it. Mike lifted the spade and tried again, this time hacking at the dirt as if he were wielding a pickaxe.

He managed to dislodge a little dirt but it was clear that the task ahead of him was going to be time-consuming.

He wiped away the sweat that had already accumulated on his brow and continued his grisly task.

Jen woke up wide-eyed and frightened, the last vestiges of a nightmare still fresh in her mind. She'd been in the woods with Sam and the earth beneath their feet had opened up, swallowing him while Jen looked on helplessly.

She looked over at the clock on the bedside table, whose glowing digits said it was almost

1:00 a.m. It was too hot in her room. She liked the hot summer days they'd been experiencing lately but the heat was a killer at night.

Certain she wouldn't be able to sleep for a while, unwilling to try in case she experienced another nightmare, she got out of bed and put on her white dressing gown. Studiously avoiding the window that looked out over the woods, she left the room and went downstairs. The lights were still on down here and she remembered that her dad was still up. Deciding to avoid a confrontation with him—they'd barely spoken since their argument over the Ouija board yesterday—she slipped her trainers on, opened the front door, and went out into the garden to get some fresh air.

The night air was warm and earthy-smelling. Jen realised she wasn't going to find it any cooler out here than inside, and since running into her dad was a real possibility, she decided to return to her room and try to find the desk fan that was packed inside one of the boxes there.

But as she turned to go back into the house, something on the road caught her attention. When she focused on it and saw that it was Sam's bike, she felt a wave of confusion wash over her. After ignoring Sam's wave and entering the house, she hadn't checked to see if he'd ridden away. Judging by the fact that the bike was parked exactly where it had been earlier, it looked like Sam had never left.

So where was he? Why had he left the bike by the side of the road?

The only reason she could think of was that the bike had broken down and Sam had left it here. But that didn't make sense. The bike was clearly his pride and joy and if it had broken down, he'd have wheeled it home or come back later to pick it up; there was no way he'd have abandoned it.

Conscious that she was wearing her dressing gown but also sure that nobody would be on the isolated road at this time of night, Jen pushed through the gate and walked along the road to where the bike was parked.

The black and gold helmet still hung from the handlebars, exactly where it had been earlier. The Norton hadn't moved since she'd seen Sam standing beside it.

So where was he? After he'd waved to Jen, if he hadn't gone home, where had he gone?

She knew the answer deep down but hardly dared admit it to herself. He'd gone into the woods in search of the house Jen had told him about.

And never returned.

She cast a glance at the trees by the side of the road but the moonlight revealed nothing. Had Sam wandered in there become lost? She doubted it; he was familiar with this area and had even said that he'd been in these woods plenty of times in the past. No, he wasn't lost; if he was still in the woods, it was because someone or something was keeping him there.

Don't jump to conclusions, she told herself. *He might have just fallen and broken his leg or something.* That theory didn't seem likely, though, because she knew Sam had his phone with him. If he'd been injured, he'd have called someone.

So what should she do? Should *she* call someone? The police? How would she explain to them that she thought Sam was a missing person merely because he'd left his bike here?

She either had to get help or go into the woods herself and look for Sam. There was no way she was doing the former—she didn't dare go into the woods in broad daylight, never mind at night—so that meant she needed help. Turning toward the house, she decided that no matter how much she'd fallen out with her dad, she was going to have to tell him about this. They had to put their differences aside; Sam's life may be in danger.

But as she took her first step towards Crow

House, a voice called her from the trees. It was Sam's voice, weak and desperate.

"Jen."

She stopped and peered into the gloom beneath the trees. Nothing moved there. "Sam? Is that you? Are you okay?"

"I need help."

Jen stepped off the road and onto the grass without hesitation but stopped there, a growing fear in her gut making it impossible to go any farther. What if it wasn't Sam calling her from the shadows but something else? She'd seen this scene from countless horror movies and it never ended well for the person responding to the cry for help.

This isn't a movie, she told herself firmly. *My friend is in trouble.*

But her feet, which had led her unwillingly toward the woods earlier, now seemed rooted to the spot, as immovable as the trees.

"Jen!" Sam urged. "Please help me."

"Why can't you come out onto the road?" she asked.

"I fell over and I can't walk. I lost my phone so I couldn't call for help."

"I'll call an ambulance," she said. "My phone is back at the house."

"No, please. Don't leave me here. I need you, Jen. I need you."

Torn between a desire to help her friend and a stark, primal terror of the woods, Jen remained frozen.

"Jen?" Sam asked pathetically, "Why are you ignoring me?"

"I'm not ignoring you, Sam, I'm thinking about what I should do."

"You should help me," he told her. "It's what any decent person would do."

As he spoke, she tried to locate his voice and decided it was coming from the shadows just a few feet away from her. She wouldn't have to go deep into the woods to find him, just a couple of steps. Then she could drag him out onto the road, into the moonlight.

"Jen?"

"I'm coming," she said.

And with those words, she stepped beneath the trees.

Mike was finally making progress. The hole in the cellar floor was at least three feet deep now and the earth, which had been hard-packed and frustratingly difficult to dig into during the first hour of his labour, was now looser and easier to penetrate with the spade.

In fact, the hole was so deep now that Mike

was beginning to doubt that Jonathan Cain's remains were down here at all. Surely he'd have found them by now. The hole that had swallowed up Cain in the dream vision hadn't been all that deep. It had been a shallow grave.

He climbed out of the hole and sat on the floor near the stairs, exhausted. His arm, leg, neck, and back muscles, which had already been aching from yesterday's gardening work, were knotted into tight fists of pain. He checked the time on his phone. Just after 2:00 a.m. If he didn't find something soon, he was going to call it a night.

A noise from upstairs caught his attention. It had sounded like the front door slamming. Certain that everyone was asleep, Mike got up and ascended the stairs, trying to ignore a cramp in his thigh. When he got to the kitchen, he peered out into the hallway and saw a flash of white there. Then he heard someone going upstairs.

Stepping into the hallway, afraid that an intruder had entered the house or that a ghostly visitor was ascending the stairs, he felt a rush of relief when he saw that the person going up to the next floor was only Jen.

She was wearing her dressing gown and trainers, which Mike thought odd, but it was the way she walked up the stairs that he found even more strange. Her arms hung limply by her sides and her actions seemed automatic, as if she were in a trance. Was she sleepwalking?

"Hey, Jen!" he shouted after her.

She ignored him and continued climbing the stairs. When she reached the landing, she turned slowly to the left and trudged to her room.

"Jen!"

Still ignoring him—or oblivious of his presence—she opened the door of her room and went inside. The door closed gently behind her.

Mike stood at the foot of the stairs and pondered whether Jen had ignored him because she'd been sleepwalking or because was still mad at him. She'd never walked in her sleep before, as far as he knew, so he put her silence down to her still being angry with him over the Ouija board thing.

But why had she been she outside?

He was sure the noise he'd heard from the cellar had been the front door closing and Jen had tracked mud into the hall and up the stairs. She'd definitely been outside.

At 2:00 a.m?

Mike opened the front door and went out into the garden, hoping to find some explanation for Jen's nocturnal wandering.

The night was warm and the air smelled

faintly of earth and chopped weeds from the work he and Terri had done yesterday. There was nothing out here to indicate why Jen had come outside.

He scanned the nearby trees and the road that stretched into the moonlit distance. Nothing. Maybe she'd just come out for some fresh air, although the air was just as warm out here as it was inside the house.

Shrugging, he went back inside and down to the cellar. Looking at the hole, he was sure it was deeper than it had been in the dream and yet he hadn't found Jonathan or the book. Maybe the dream had been just a dream and nothing more and he'd wasted the last two hours and given himself enough aches and pains to last a lifetime in the process.

Or maybe the earth had swallowed Jonathan Cain and the *Daemones Mortum* over the years, pulling both man and book deeper into its grip, unwilling to relinquish its prize.

Mike decided to give it another twenty minutes and then he'd go to bed. If he was still able to wield the spade tomorrow without agonizing pain, he'd resume digging tomorrow night.

Grabbing the spade and climbing reluctantly into the hole, he set about pushing the blade into the soft dirt and shoveling it out onto the cellar floor.

Five minutes later, the spade contacted something that was harder than the surrounding earth. Mike heard the object *click* against the metal blade. He threw down the spade and got to his hands and knees, scrabbling in the dirt with his bare hands.

His searching fingers uncovered a patch of white among the dark soil. Swallowing hard, he brushed away more dirt and revealed the top of a skull, its eye sockets filled with earth.

He backed away from it and sat down, letting out a long breath. Here was the proof that the dream had been more than just a fanciful wandering of his mind. Here was the skeleton of Jonathan Cain and Mike was sure that he would find the *Daemones Mortum* clutched in its dead hands.

Finding the skeleton, more than anything else that had happened to him, confirmed to Mike that everything regarding the ghost of Cain haunting Crow House was real. That meant everything else must be real too: the sacrifices left in the woods for the demon, the witches who were drowned in the lake centuries ago, and the very real danger that his family was in.

From the position of the skull, he tried to

figure out where the skeleton's chest might be and began using his hands to dig in that area. A minute later, he touched something leathery and at first recoiled, thinking it might be Jonathan Cain's flesh. But as he regained his nerve, he brushed away more dirt to reveal the flat cover of a book.

Uncovering it completely, Mike pried the leather-bound book from Jonathan Cain's skeletal hands and placed it on the cellar floor while he climbed out of the grave. Looking down at the exposed skull and hands of the man who had lived in this house in Victorian times—a man whose ghost had visited Mike and led him to the grave—he felt a tinge of sadness.

Jonathan Cain had come to Crow House with his wife and daughter for a new start, away from the city. But instead of starting a new chapter in their lives, the family had found only death. Were the bodies of Mary and Elizabeth buried in similar shallow graves, perhaps in the woods? Mike had no idea about that but one thing he was sure of was that he wouldn't let that happen to his family. Terri, Jen, and Chris weren't going to end up buried in the woods or under the house. He refused to let that happen.

The *Daemones Mortum* had the power to

banish the demon, according to Eric Maxwell and Mike was determined to use it to do just that.

He filled in the grave as quickly as he could and began to read the book.

20

DAEMONES MORTUM

July 31st

Mike reached the little house in the woods and stole inside, quickly shutting the door behind him. During his journey here, he'd been sure he was being watched but couldn't see or hear anyone else in the woods. He'd stopped to look around a few times but as far as he could tell, he'd been alone. So why had he felt as if strange faces were peeking around the trees at him when his back was turned?

Now that he was in the house, he felt a little more relaxed. He quickly climbed the steps to the upper room, where he'd left the box containing Jonathan Cain's letters and books, as well as Wendy Maxwell's diary.

Last night, after filling in the grave in the cellar, he'd leafed through the *Daemones Mortum* until he'd come to the page where Cain had placed the bookmark. Mike had feared that a hundred years buried in dirt might have rotted the pages but had soon discovered that the pages of the *Daemones Mortum* weren't made of paper at all, but thin sheets of leather. He didn't want to dwell on the possible origins of that leather.

The section of the book where Cain had thrust the bookmark was concerned with a spell to banish "a forest-dwelling daemon that preys on good souls." Cain had obviously determined that this banishment was appropriate for the demon in these woods. The spell itself seemed simple enough, nothing more than a fire that was to be lit in the woods within a salt circle, a few symbols that were to be traced in the air with a stick from the "woods where the daemon dwells" and a paragraph of strange words that had to be recited from the *Daemones Mortum*.

The book also stated that the banisher must wear a protective talisman. Mike had no problem there; he'd been wearing Jonathan Cain's talisman since the day he'd found it.

The next condition described in the *Daemones Mortum* gave him pause. The book said that "the banisher must know and speak the true name of the daemon" and there were blank spaces in the wording of the spell where the banisher was supposed to say the demon's name.

Mike had no idea what the name was but hoped to find the answer in Jonathan Cain's journal. Cain had taken it upon himself to research the occult, so he must have found out the demon's name.

He sat on the bed frame and placed the box between his feet, digging Cain's journal out from beneath the letters and the diary and opening it on his lap. Jonathan Cain's handwriting flowed neatly across the pages, describing at first mundane details about daily life at Crow House. It seemed the family had at first enjoyed their new life in the countryside but as Mike turned the pages and read on, it became obvious that Cain's concern regarding his wife's behaviour eventually grew into an obsession.

Mike couldn't decipher exactly what it was about Mary's behaviour that convinced Jonathan his wife was a witch—the journal was vague on this point—but it seemed that Jonathan had taken up the study of magic to deliver his family from the "evil that has befallen us."

An entry from June 1892 caught Mike's eye.

I do not know the demon's true name, as required by the spell book. Mary knows it, of course, but will not speak it. I must do everything within my power to discover that name. The book describes a Shroud of Truth. I must make a shroud and emblazon it with the necessary symbols. Then I must cover Mary with it while she is shackled and question her about the demon's name.

Mike glanced at the manacles attached to the bed frame. The entry explained why Jonathan had imprisoned his wife in this room and tried to exorcise the evil from her; he was attempting to learn the demon's name so that he could banish it for good.

It seemed he'd failed in that task because Mike couldn't find any name in the journal and the entries abruptly ended on July 31st, 1892.

He placed the journal back into the box, frustrated with the little knowledge it had imparted. If Jonathan Cain had been unable to glean the demon's name from torturing his wife, then how was Mike supposed to discover it now, a century later?

Without the name, he couldn't cast the spell. The Gule of August was tomorrow and if Eric Maxwell was right, the demon would claim another victim on that day.

He remembered Wendy Maxwell's diary.

She'd been possessed, apparently in the same way Mary Cain had been, so maybe she'd known the demon's name. She'd scrawled a strange word in the last pages of the diary. Was that the answer Jonathan Cain had been seeking all those years earlier?

Mike picked up the diary and flipped to the last page.

Gethsemiel.

The words had obviously been important to Wendy Maxwell because she'd written it repeatedly in the diary. The last few pages were covered with it, as if Wendy hadn't been able to think or write anything else.

Had she written the name down because she was hoping someone would use it to banish the demon and save her?

Mike placed the diary into the box and put his face in his hands, considering his next step. If Gethsemiel was indeed the name of the demon, then he had all the ingredients needed to cast the banishment.

One simple question niggled him: He *could* cast the banishment but *should* he?

He didn't know anything about magic, the occult, ghosts, or demons and he had the feeling that he was playing with fire. The book said the talisman would protect him from the power of the spell but could he really trust the book? For all he knew, everything within its pages was nothing more than mumbo-jumbo. Just because Jonathan Cain had trusted in the *Daemones Mortum* didn't mean it was the genuine article.

Wouldn't Mike's best course of action be to forget about the whole thing and get his family out of here?

The thought brought with it a pang of guilt. This demon had taken victims from these woods for centuries and now, for the first time, the method to destroy it was at hand. If Mike ignored that, he could be sentencing more people to death. The demon would continue to feed on anyone who came to this area. And that meant that tomorrow, on the Gule of August, someone else would die.

But at least it won't be a member of my family.

He reasoned that he could give both the book and the talisman to Eric Maxwell and let him sort it out. There might even be some sort of poetic justice in that because Eric could banish the demon and avenge his brother.

And while Eric was doing that, Mike would take his family far away from here, at least for a few days. They'd have to return to Crow House after that but by then the danger should be gone if Eric performed the banishment correctly.

He went back downstairs, decided. He'd give the magic paraphernalia to Eric Maxwell and get his family out of here. They'd stay at a cheap hotel for a couple of days and return to Crow House after that.

As he went outside and stepped off the porch, he noticed an aberration in the trunk of the huge oak tree that grew next to the house. It looked as if the ancient tree's bark was bulging out near ground level. Mike was sure it hadn't been like that before, although he hadn't looked at the tree when he'd entered the house because he'd been too busy scanning the woods for unseen faces watching him.

He went over to investigate and took a shocked step backward when he realised the bulge was shaped like a man.

Taking a step closer, he could clearly see the shape of the face, its features caught in a scream as the man's hands pushed against the bark, as if trying to reach out from inside the tree.

The thin layer of bark that covered the man's form had moulded itself to every feature of his face. Mike was sure this was Sam, the young man who'd driven Jen home the other day. How had he ended up here, like this? It was as if he'd suffered a similar fate to Jonathan Cain but instead of being buried alive in the dirt, Sam had been swallowed alive by the tree.

Was he alive in there? Mike reached out and ran his fingertips over the bark that encased the silently screaming face.

He can't be alive, he told himself. *That would be impossible.*

Not too long ago, you'd have thought it impossible that a demon lives in these woods.

Mike stepped away from the oak. This confirmed his decision to get the hell out of here. There was no way he could fight an evil entity that could entomb people inside trees.

The best thing to do right now was to get back to the house, tell everyone to pack their things, and leave Crow House immediately.

He needed to get Terri, Chris, and Jen as far away from here as possible. He wasn't sure how he was going to do that without arousing suspicion but he couldn't have them here on the Gule of August under any circumstances. He wasn't going to let his own family end up like the Cains or the Maxwells. He couldn't bear to see Jen's screaming face bulging from a tree like a grotesque carving, or watch Chris being buried alive by an unseen force.

They had to leave. Now.

He turned away from the oak tree and fled through the trees toward Crow House.

21

PENTAGRAM

THE FIRST THING Jen became aware of as she woke up was a stinging pain on her right wrist. She sat up in bed and pulled her arm from beneath the covers, alarmed when she saw blood.

A dark red, roughly circular patch of dried, flaky blood covered the inside of her wrist. The skin stung as if Jen had cut herself but the encrusted blood hid any wounds beneath.

Getting out of bed, surprised to find she still had her shoes on, Jen rushed along the hall to the bathroom and put her hand beneath the cold tap, wincing as the water touched her skin.

As the dried blood moistened and fell away from her wrist, she saw with horror that she had indeed cut herself but instead of the single cut she'd expected to find, five slashes ran across her skin to form a pentagram.

She closed her eyes, both to hide the mutilation from her sight and to try and remember what had happened last night. She recalled going outside to get some air and seeing Sam's bike on the road. She'd gone over to it and heard his voice calling for help. And then…

And then what? She had no idea what had happened after she'd stepped into the woods. If it weren't for the pentagram carved into her wrist, she'd have assumed the night uneventful.

But something had happened during the period of time she couldn't remember. The five slashes in her arm confirmed that. Had she done this to herself or had someone else cut that pattern into her skin?

She turned off the tap and searched in the box marked "Bathroom" for the bandages they'd brought from the London flat. She found one and bound her wrist tightly before returning to her room and finding a long-sleeved top that would hide the bandage but also not be too stifling in the summer heat.

When she was dressed appropriately, she went downstairs, where she could hear her mum and Chris talking and eating lunch in the kitchen. She needed to see if Sam's bike was still parked on the road. If it was, she'd find the number of the Wetherby family and call them. She needed to know if Sam was okay.

She stepped out into the front garden and shielded her eyes against the bright sun as she searched the road for the bike. It was gone. Jen felt a flood of relief. Her theory about the bike breaking down and Sam coming back to collect it seemed possible now. And if Sam had taken the bike, that meant he was okay.

But that didn't explain how she'd heard his voice last night, calling to her from the shadows beneath the trees. Those shadows drew her gaze now and she started, shocked, when she saw a dark figure standing beneath the trees. It was too far away to make out any details but one thing she was certain of was that it wasn't Sam. It was much too tall be him or any person at all for that matter.

The figure stood so still that she might have thought it no more than a tall shadow except for the two bright eyes that seemed to be staring directly at her.

Jen took an involuntary step backward on the lawn and her heart began to hammer against her ribs. The tall, dark figure regarded her calmly, its eyes two shiny pinpoints of light as if the sun were reflecting off two bottle caps or pieces of glass.

The pentagram on Jen's wrist began to

throb with each beat of her racing heart and she realised with sudden despair that the symbol tied her somehow to that dark figure beneath the trees. She was also convinced that she'd made the cuts herself, to mark herself as belonging to the bright-eyed creature.

"No," she said, shaking her head, certain that it could hear her even though it was so far away and her words were barely more than a whisper. "I didn't mean to mark myself. You made me do it."

The figure didn't reply, simply watched her with those reflective eyes and although the dual pinpricks of light conveyed no emotion, Jen felt like a helpless mouse being preyed upon by a ravenous hawk.

She turned back to the house and ran inside.

"Are you okay, Jen?" her mother called from the kitchen.

"Fine," she called back, going into the living room and peering through the window. Her eyes found the place in the trees where she'd seen the figure but all she could see now were ordinary shadows.

Jen turned from the window and went into the kitchen where her mother and brother were still eating. "We have to leave," she said, her voice breaking as tears sprung from her eyes.

Her mum went to her and drew her into her arms. "Don't worry, we will. As soon as we get enough money together, we're out of here."

"No," Jen said, holding her mother tight, "we have to get out of this house right now."

"You know we can't do that," her mum said softly. "Everything will be back to normal soon and this place will be nothing more than a memory. Okay?"

Jen pulled away from her. Why was everyone in her family oblivious to what was going on around here? "You don't get it! This place is haunted and we need to leave right now. We're not safe here!"

"Haunted?" her mum said, trying to suppress a chuckle. "Now you're starting to sound like your brother."

Jen spun on her heels and stormed up to her room, slamming the door behind her. She sprawled onto her bed, burying her face into the pillow, letting the tears flow. Nobody ever listened to her. She felt trapped in this house and even though her family was right here with her, she felt more alone than he'd ever felt in her entire life.

At least once the summer was over, she'd be at college in London, far away from this damned place. She sat up on the bed and pulled up her sleeve so she could see the bandage around her wrist.

What makes you think you're going to live through the summer? You've been marked for that thing in the woods and when the time is right, it'll come to take you.

That thought scared her and she tried shaking it out of her head but it made its home there, niggling at her.

We have to get out of here. If Mum won't listen to me, maybe I can convince Dad.

She rejected that idea immediately. Trying to convince her dad that a creature inhabited the woods was never going to work. He was the most rational person she knew and there was no way he'd believe anything regarding strange creatures or the supernatural.

She had to think of some other way to get her family out of Crow House and away from the woods.

Just as she began trying to come up with an idea, the door downstairs opened and then slammed shut and she heard her dad in the kitchen, speaking in a panicked voice. Jen got off the bed and opened her door, stepping out onto the landing so she could hear what her father was saying. She'd never heard him sound so scared.

As she leaned over the bannister to hear

better, his words made her feel like she had a chance of surviving the summer after all.

Her dad was talking to her mom and Chris, saying, "Grab your things and pack a suitcase. We're getting out of here now."

22

THE TRAP

When Mike burst into the kitchen and said they were leaving, the last person he expected to object was his wife. But Terri folded her arms, shook her head, and said, "We're not going anywhere."

"You don't understand," he told her, "We're in danger here. We have to go right now."

Terri looked incredulous. "Is this a prank, Mike? Because it isn't funny."

"I'm being serious. We have to leave. Right now."

She laughed and he sensed irritation and anger in the sound. "Why? What's changed your mind all of a sudden?"

"I can't explain it," he said, knowing that if he told her about the demon, she'd think he'd finally tipped over the edge into madness.

"But we're supposed to just pack up and leave without an explanation?"

"You're just going to have to trust me on this, Terri."

She shook her head. "No, Mike, I'm not. You dragged us all the way up here from London and now you expect us to drop everything and leave just because you say so? No, it doesn't work that way. We're here now and we're staying."

Mike had no idea why Terri would want to stay in a house she professed to hate unless she was so being so obstinate that she'd do anything as long as it was the opposite of what he, Mike, wanted. He supposed he couldn't blame her for that but there was a lot at stake and this was no time to play games. "Terri, I don't have time to explain. Grab what you need, we're getting out of here."

In defiance, she sat down at the table next to Chris. "I told you, I'm staying. Unless you can give me a damn good reason to leave, I'm staying right here."

He threw up his hands in frustration. "What do you want me to say? That there's a demon in the woods and it wants our family? That the ghost of a man whose wife and daughter were possessed by that demon haunts this house?

Because that's what's happening here, Terri, and I'm trying to protect you from it."

She frowned at him, shaking her head. "I'd expect this kind of talk from Chris but not from you. You've never believed in ghosts, demons, or anything like that. You're too level-headed."

"Which is why you have to listen to me now. I wouldn't be saying this if it weren't true. There's a demon in those woods and it's real, Terri. It isn't a story or a legend, it's real."

She cocked an eyebrow. "As real as the face in that photo you took?"

Mike sighed. He knew that as far as Terri was concerned, he was hallucinating or losing his mind.

"Dad's telling the truth," Chris said. "We were talking to an old man who told us about the demon. It takes a victim every year on the first day of August."

Terri turned her attention to her son. "What man?"

Mike could see this was going to make things worse but he couldn't do anything to stop Chris saying what he was about to say next.

"Eric Maxwell," Chris told his mother. "His brother lived in this house in the 70s and he killed his wife and daughter because he thought they were witches."

Terri shot an accusing look at Mike. "What the hell, Mike? You let our son talk with the brother of a murderer?"

"It isn't like that," he told her, already sensing that this was going to lead to another argument. There was no way Terri was going to leave Crow House now. Even if she believed there was a demon in the woods, she'd stay just to spite Mike.

Jen appeared in the doorway, her eyes red-rimmed and her face tired. "Mum, you need to listen to Dad. We have to leave this house. There's a creature in the woods. I've seen it."

"Now see what you've done?" Terri shouted at Mike. "You've got your children believing in monsters. You need help, Mike. Professional help." She got up from the table and sighed. "I'll be in my studio if anyone needs me. One of us has to do some work if we're ever going to get back on our feet again." She left the kitchen and went upstairs.

"What are we going to do, Dad?" Jen asked.

"We're getting out of here," he told her.

"But we can't leave Mum," Chris said.

"We won't. I'll find a way to convince her to come with us." But even as he said the words, he didn't have much confidence in them.

"I could show her this," Jen said, pulling back a bandage on her arm.

When Mike saw the pentagram sliced into her skin, he felt fear grip his heart. "How did you get that?"

"I don't remember exactly. I think I did it to myself but not because I wanted to. It made me do it."

The fist around his heart tightened as Mike remembered those same words coming from the mouth of Eliza Cain. His daughter was obviously connected to the demon somehow, marked by it. Did that mean she was its intended victim on August 1st?

"Don't show that to your mum," he told Jen. "It's only going to worry her. For now, we need to figure out how we're going to get everyone—your mum included—out of this house. At least for a few days."

"We could knock her out with chloroform and bundle her into the car," Chris suggested. Mike hoped his son was trying to be humorous.

"I'll talk to her," he said. "You two go and pack for a couple of days in a hotel."

Jen and Chris went upstairs while Mike remained in the kitchen, thinking about what he was going to say to Terri. There was no point mentioning demons or ghosts because she clearly thought that was nonsense. If he was going to get her to leave the house, he needed a rational reason for her to do so.

After racking his brain for a couple of minutes, he decided to appeal to his wife's better nature. If he told her that Chris and Jen were frightened to stay at the house, surely she'd leave for their sake.

He went upstairs to find the door of her studio closed. Now that he thought about it, she'd kept this room private ever since moving her painting materials inside. In London, she'd set up her easel in the corner of the kitchen and painted there, sometimes while Mike watched. He loved to watch her work, her entire focus concentrated on the canvas in front of her. And Terri had allowed him to watch, sometimes putting on a fake Bob Ross voice and narrating what she was doing.

But since they'd arrived at Crow House, her work had been carried out behind closed doors. Mike guessed it was just another way she was punishing him for putting them into this situation.

He knocked lightly on the door and was surprised to hear, after few seconds, a key turn in the lock. Was she locking herself in there as well?

The door opened a crack and her face appeared, the familiar resigned look sitting on her features like a heavy mask. "What do you want, Mike?"

"Look, I get that you're angry at me and you don't want to leave here because it's my idea. But the kids are really upset and they want to spend a couple of days away from here."

"That's because you've been filling their heads with nonsense."

He shrugged. Denial at this point would only lead to another argument and Terri would probably close and lock the door. "Whatever the reason, the point is, they're scared. They don't want to stay here. So how about I book a hotel for a couple of days? We can even go back to London if you like, visit some of our old haunts."

She looked at him seriously. "Is that supposed to be funny?"

"What?"

"Haunts."

"No, it's just a word. I didn't mean—"

"Save it, Mike. We're not going anywhere." She slammed the door and he heard the key turn in the lock.

Knowing it was pointless talking to her while she was in this mood, he went into their bedroom and threw his suitcase onto the bed before stuffing clothes into it. Terri might be being stubborn at the moment but he couldn't let anything get in the way of keeping his family safe. Crow House and the surrounding woods were dangerous. He had to get everyone away from that danger.

Jen was selecting clothes from her wardrobe and placing them into her suitcase when she heard a tap at the window. She turned to look but there was no one there.

Of course no one's there. This room is on the top floor.

As she pondered that, a small stone hit the pane and bounced off it. Jen went to the window and looked down, thinking Chris was playing a trick on her.

But the person she saw standing beyond the back gate wasn't Chris at all. It was Sam, dressed in the same Pink Floyd T-shirt he'd been wearing yesterday. He was staring up at her window and when he saw her, he gave her a slight wave.

Jen felt as if her heart were about to burst. Sam was okay! Her worry over his disappearance had been pointless. She threw open the window and called, "I'll be there in a minute," before checking herself in the mirror and rushing downstairs.

When she reached the gate, though, Sam wasn't there.

She turned and checked the bushes in the garden, wondering if Sam planned to jump out and surprise her but he wasn't anywhere to be seen. Besides, he'd been standing by the lake when she'd seen him from her window and she'd come down straight away so he'd hardly have time to come in through the gate and hide.

So where was he?

She opened the gate and looked around. When she finally spotted Sam, he was standing at the edge of the woods, half-obscured by the shadows there.

Jen waved at him to join her by the gate. There was no way she was going anywhere near the woods.

He mimicked her action, waving for her to go to him.

She shook her head and waved at him again.

He did the same.

Jen sighed. Why did boys have to be so stupid sometimes? "Stop playing games," she called to him. "Come over here."

He shook his head and sat down on the ground, arms folded.

"Fine," she called. "I'm going back inside. See ya." She turned back to the gate, hoping he'd call her name to stop her. As she put a hand on the iron gate, Sam called her but his voice sounded funny, as if his throat was dry or something.

"Jen." It was almost a croak.

She stopped and turned to face him. He was standing again now, and waving her over.

She hesitated. What harm would it do to go to the edge of the woods where Sam was standing? She wouldn't have to actually go into the woods. And once she was face to face with him, she could tell him that she wanted to talk over here by the house.

She took a few steps toward him and he stopped waving at her. Now, he stood stock still, arms hanging limply by his sides, as he watched her approach.

Jen stopped. Something didn't feel right. Sam was acting weirdly. She glanced over her shoulder and realised she'd ventured farther from the gate than she'd thought.

"Come and talk in the house," she called to Sam.

He didn't answer, merely began waving at her again.

"This isn't funny," she told him, walking toward him again. She was going to tell him off for scaring her when she was face to face with him.

But as she got nearer, Sam turned and walked into the woods, his back to her.

"No, wait!" she called after him.

If he heard her, he didn't respond. He didn't stop either.

"Sam, come back!"

He'd almost disappeared into the shadows now but seemed to be walking slow enough that he wouldn't vanish completely from her sight, as if he were enticing her into the trees.

Before she realised it, Jen was in the woods running after him. She had to know what had happened after she'd left him by the side of the road and the only way to know that was to talk to him. Breathless, she called his name but he didn't stop.

And she followed him deeper into the woods.

23

MISSING PERSON

Mike was sitting in the living room, searching on his laptop for London hotels, when he heard a car pull up outside the house. He peeked out of the window and sighed when he saw DCI Battle's green Land Rover parked by the gate. DCI Battle and DS Lyons were climbing out of the vehicle.

"What the hell do they want?" Mike mumbled. He'd finished packing an hour ago but Chris and Jen still hadn't come out of their rooms. Jen he could understand because she was probably second-guessing every item of clothing she put in her suitcase but Chris shouldn't have taken this long to throw a few T-shirts into his case.

What really irked him, though, was the fact that Terri was still locked inside her studio. It wasn't as if she were sitting across the room sulking. At least then he could gauge her mood. But as long as she was behind the locked door, no communication was possible and he had no idea if she was still angry with him or just working on one of her paintings.

The arrival of the police did nothing to lighten his own mood.

He went to the front door and opened it just as DS Lyons was about to knock. She lowered hand and gave him a brief smile. "Good afternoon, sir, we were wondering if you've seen this young man in the area recently." She held up a photo of Sam. In the picture, he was leaning on a black and gold Norton motorbike and grinning from ear to ear. A sign behind him read *Easton's Garage*.

"That's Sam Wetherby," Battle said. "He didn't come home last night and no one can get in contact with him so his mother called us. The motorbike is also missing."

Mike wasn't sure what to say. If he told the police that he knew where Sam was, that would raise questions. On the other hand, if he said he hadn't seen Sam, the boy's family might never know what had become of him. For all Mike knew, the huge oak tree was absorbing Sam's body and all trace of the boy might soon be gone. Only he, Mike, would know what had become of the poor lad. Was he willing to have that on his conscience?

"Sir?" Lyons asked.

Mike sighed. If he covered up the fact that he knew where the boy was, how would he ever live with himself? But how could he explain to the police that he'd seen Sam Wetherby inside a tree?

"There's something you need to see," he said.

Battle and Lyons suddenly looked alert. "Do you know Sam Wetherby's whereabouts?" Lyons asked.

"Like I said, I need to show you," Mike said, aware that his cryptic answer wasn't doing him any favours but sure that when they saw the boy in the tree, the detectives would understand why Mike had to show them and couldn't merely explain what he knew.

"Lead the way then, sir," Battle said.

Mike put on his boots and led the two detectives through the house and out through the back door. When he saw the woods, he felt a momentary sense of dread creep through his body like a cold tentacle but forced himself to ignore it and walk steadily toward the trees.

The detectives walked silently on either side of him, their faces betraying no emotion at all.

The cool shadows of the woods fell over them as they reached the trees and Mike took them to the oak tree that sat next to the ramshackle house. "He's in there," he told them.

"In the house?" Battle asked as he and Lyons stepped up onto the front porch.

"No, in the tree."

Battle and Lyons exchanged a look.

"The tree," Mike repeated, going over to the huge oak. "He's inside the—" He bit back his words when he saw that the oak's bark was smooth. There was no sign of the Sam-shaped lump that had been there earlier. "I don't understand. He was here. Right here in the tree."

Battle approached Mike warily and put a gentle hand on his shoulder. "Are you all right, sir?"

Mike shook the detective's hand off and ran his own hands over the smooth tree trunk. "I was here earlier and I saw Sam Wetherby inside this tree."

"Inside the tree, sir?"

"Inside the tree," Mike repeated.

"Are you sure you weren't mistaken?"

"No, I wasn't mistaken. I saw him as clearly as I can see you now."

"As clearly as you saw that face in the window the other day?" Lyons asked, coming out of the house onto the porch. She directed her attention to Battle. "Wetherby isn't in the house, guv."

"I'm not crazy," Mike said. "I know how this looks, especially after what happened the last time, but I'm telling you, Sam Wetherby was inside that tree."

"Yet you didn't report it," Lyons shot back.

"If he was inside the tree," Battle said, running a finger over the smooth bark, "he didn't cause any damage when he got out."

Lyons chuckled.

"This isn't a joke," Mike said, pointing an accusing finger at Battle. "You're the one who told me the house was haunted."

"I didn't tell you the house was haunted, sir."

"You said these woods a bad place and that people go missing here all the time. Like the Bermuda Triangle, with Crow House in the centre of it."

Battle nodded. "That's a fact. People have disappeared from here a lot over the years. And some bad things have happened in that house, that's undeniable. But you're telling me you saw Sam Wetherby inside a tree, only he isn't here now, as we can all see. If you have some evidence…"

"No, I don't have any evidence."

"And as DS Lyons said, you didn't report what you saw to the police. Surely, if you thought someone was stuck inside a tree, you'd give us a call."

"I was scared," Mike admitted. "I ran home and told my family to pack their things. We're going to spend a few days in London."

Battle grimaced. "I'm afraid that won't be possible, sir."

"Why? What do you mean?"

"We have a boy missing from the area and you've told us that you know something about it. I can't let you go swanning off to the city now, can I?"

"But I don't know anything about it, I was wrong. I obviously didn't see what I thought I saw. Like that face in the photo."

Battle shook his head. "Sorry, sir, but there's a bit more to it than that. Our enquiries have revealed that Sam was last seen riding his motorbike along the road that leads past your house."

"You didn't tell me that."

"No I didn't. You seemed eager to show us something that I didn't get the chance."

Mike wished he'd kept his mouth shut.

"May we have a word with your daughter, sir? We have reason to believe Sam was coming here to visit her."

"Yes, of course," Mike said. Refusal to let them speak to Jen would only ignite their suspicion further and that was the last thing he needed. But there was one thing of which he was certain: he and his family would be leaving here today whether the police liked it or not. There was too much at stake. He'd rather face Battle's wrath later than have his family ripped apart by a demon.

"Lead the way, sir," Battle said cheerily, indicating the way back to Crow House.

Mike led them back to the house in silence.

When they were in the hallway, he shouted up the stairs for Jen to come down.

"Jen!" he called again when she didn't show.

Chris came out of his room and poked his head over the bannister. "What's up, Dad?"

"Tell your sister to get down here."

Chris sighed as if he'd been given a monumental task and then disappeared. He reappeared a moment later. "She's not in her room."

"What do you mean she's not in her room? She was supposed to be packing."

"Yeah, her case is on her bed with some clothes and stuff in it."

"I'm sorry," Mitch said to Battle, "she doesn't seem to be here at the moment."

"No problem, sir, we have other lines of enquiry to follow. Perhaps you could give me a call when your daughter gets home. You have my card." He turned to the front door and opened it but before stepping outside, he turned to Mike and said, "I'm going to have to insist that you don't leave the area, at least until Sam turns up."

"Fine," Mike said. He had more pressing concerns than Battle's instruction. Where the hell was Jen? Why would she leave the house on her own?

Battle looked past Mike, into the kitchen, and said, "Ah, here she is."

Mike turned to see Jen coming from the kitchen. A questioning look crossed her face as she noticed the detectives.

"Miss Wilson," Battle said, all smiles now, "can you tell me if you saw Sam Wetherby yesterday?"

"No," Jen said, shaking her head. "He hasn't been here."

Battle's smile turned into a frown. "Are you sure? According to his sister, he was coming out here to visit you."

"I just told you I haven't seen him," Jen said.

"The last time you spoke, did he tell you of any plans he had to leave the area? Visit friends elsewhere, perhaps? Any reason why he didn't arrive home last night?"

"I barely know Sam," Jen told the detective. "He gave me a lift once, that's all."

"All right," Battle said, obviously realising

that he was getting nowhere. "Well if you think of anything, let us know."

After the detectives had left, Mike closed the front door and turned to face Jen. "Where have you been?"

"Just outside to get some air."

Mike found that strange. Why would she abandon her packing to go outside? "Is your suitcase ready?"

She shook her head. "I've been thinking about it and I think Mum is right. We shouldn't abandon this place for no reason. We only just got here so we should stay a while longer."

"There is a reason," Mike told her. "You said yourself that you saw a creature in the woods. Those cuts on your arm—"

"Everybody cuts themselves these days," she said lightly. "Is it surprising with all the stress I've been under? I'll be in my room in anyone needs me." She swung herself playfully around the newel post at the bottom of the bannister and ascended the stairs.

As Mike watched her go, he felt a sense of dread tighten across his chest. The demon in the woods had possessed his daughter; there was no doubting that any longer.

He went up to Chris's room and knocked on the door before entering. Chris was closing his suitcase, pressing down on the hard-shell lid with one hand while trying to zip up the case with the other. Mike could see that the case was mostly filled with books about strange creatures and conspiracy theories.

He helped Chris close it and then said, "We need to go to Matlock again. Right now."

"What for?"

"I'll tell you when we get there." Mike didn't feel able to speak freely here, as if the house were listening. He didn't dare speak his plan until he and Chris were far beyond these walls.

"Okay," Chris said, shrugging. He walked to the bedroom door in a manner that meant he was tired, bored, or sulking; shoulders slumped, feet dragging on the carpet.

Mike grabbed the case and hefted it out of the room and down the stairs. He found himself walking quietly past Jen's bedroom, as if he were afraid to alert her that he and Chris were leaving. Just as he couldn't let Crow House know of his plans, neither could he let Jen know what he was doing. She was the enemy now, either working for the demon or possessed by it.

When he and Chris got downstairs, Mike opened the front door as quietly as he could and led his son to the Sportage. Once they were inside the vehicle, with Chris's suitcase on the backseat, Mike let out a breath he hadn't realised he was holding. He started the engine and reversed onto the road so that the car was facing Shawby. Then he put his foot down and watched Crow House diminish in size in the rearview mirror.

Only when the house had completely disappeared from view did Mike turn to Chris and say, "There's something I need to do. And I need you to be far away from the house while I do it. You're going to stay in Matlock tonight."

Chris looked alarmed. "What do you mean? What about Mum and Jen?"

"I'll try to get them out of the house later. For now, I need to know that at least you're safe. So I'm going to book a room at a hotel and you're going to stay there tonight, okay?"

Chris eyed him closely. "Dad, what the hell is going on? Is it the demon? Tell me what's happening."

Mike knew he owed his son an explanation. If his plan went wrong, then this might be the last time he ever saw Chris. He choked back the emotions that came with that realisation and said, "I wanted all of us to leave the house and together. I was going to turn my back on that thing in the woods and just keep my family safe." He took a deep breath to steady his voice. "But I can't do that now. I think it's got Jen. So I have to fight the demon. There's a spell that banishes it and I have to cast it at midnight because tomorrow, on the first day of August, the demon takes its victim and I think that victim is your sister."

Chris's eyes widened. "The Gule of August, just like Eric Maxwell said!"

Mike nodded. "After I get you to safety, I'm going to go back for your mum and Jen. Maybe they'll listen to me, maybe not, but I'm going to try to convince them to leave."

"Then we'll all stay at the hotel, right? You too?"

Mike hesitated. That had been his original plan and it was tempting to think that he could run to the hotel and everything would be okay. But he knew deep down that he couldn't do that. The demon had its sights on Jen, had inhabited her or was controlling her somehow, and running away wasn't going to change that. He had to get rid of the damned thing once and for all if he was going to seize his daughter from its clutches.

"I need to perform the banishment," he told Chris. "I have to save Jen."

24

SHADOW IN THE MIST

THE TRAVELLER'S Inn in Matlock was clean, tidy, and cheap. After Mike had booked a room for the night and stashed the keycard in his wallet, he took Chris to the local supermarket and stocked up on enough food so that his son wouldn't have any need to leave the room. He also bought every bag of salt that he could get his hands on.

When they got back to the hotel, they unloaded the food and took it to Chris's room. As Mike placed the suitcase in the room, he took Chris gently by the shoulders. "I need you to stay in this room until I come back, okay?"

"With Mum and Jen?"

Mike nodded. "Yes, with your mother and Jen. But until then, sit tight, watch TV, or read a book. You have plenty of them in your suitcase."

"Okay," Chris said.

Mike handed him the keycard. "I love you, Chris."

"I love you too, Dad."

Mike left the hotel and climbed into the Sportage. Sitting behind the wheel and staring at the sun reflecting off the windows of the Traveller's Inn, he hesitated before starting the engine. What would happen to Chris if Mike failed to return? If the demon got him, along with Terri and Jen?

He supposed that his Uncle Rob, the closest relation Chris had, would take care of the boy.

"Uncle Rob," he muttered to himself. How much did Rob know about Crow House and why had he lied when he said he'd never been there? Eric Maxwell had said Rob had spent two weeks in the house. Of course, Maxwell could be lying but for what purpose? For that matter, why would Rob lie?

Taking out his phone, Mike found Rob's number and called it.

Rob answered after two rings. "Hey, Mike, how's country life treating you?"

"Not so great," Mike said.

Rob's voice became serious. "There's nothing wrong with the house, is there? Don't tell me they screwed me over and sold me a pig in a poke just because I wasn't there in person."

"The house is fine," Mike said. "You got a great bargain."

"Well that's a relief. So what's up?"

"Actually, I wanted to ask you something related to what you just said. You've never seen the house, right?"

"That's right," Rob said. He sounded a little wary.

"It's just that there's a guy in the village who swore to me that you stayed there for a couple of weeks after you bought it. He said he spoke to you while you were there."

"Hmmm," Rob said.

"Hmmm?" Mike asked.

"Funny thing," Rob said, "is that after I bought the house, I did make plans to go and take a look at it. I even wrote about it on my travel blog and told my readers I was going to visit a house I'd bought as an investment."

He paused and when he spoke again, there was confusion in his voice. "The thing is, I'm not exactly sure what happened next. I flew to England and hired a car, I know that much. But then my memory kind of goes hazy. The next thing I remember clearly is driving back to London and catching a flight home."

"You don't remember seeing the house? Staying there?"

"No," Rob said after a short pause. "After I got home, I went to see a doctor, told him I'd some lost time. He did some tests but everything was normal. And I've never had any loss of memory since so I just put it down as one of those things."

"So you could have visited the house," Mike said.

"Oh, I did visit the house," Rob said. "I uploaded a photo of it to my blog just before I went inside. So I know I was there. But for a couple of weeks? No, I'm sure that can't be right. I'd remember *something* if I was there for two weeks, right?"

"I don't know," Mike said. "Did you upload anything else to your blog during those two weeks after you posted the picture of the house?"

"No, there are fifteen days where I just went quiet. My followers wondered what the hell had happened to me. Then, when I posted again after I got home, I told them I'd been ill and unable to post. They forgot about the house and so did I until I heard you needed a place to stay."

Mike mulled that over for a few moments. What the hell had happened to Rob during those two weeks while he'd been at the house? Had he been into the woods? "When you offered to let us stay there," he asked, "you suggested we move in on July 25th, do you remember that?"

"Yeah, I do. I remember it clearly because you asked me when you could move in and I remember thinking *July 25th* straight away. That date just popped into my head but I felt like I *had* to get you to move in on that day and I have no idea why."

"I see," Mike said. "Well I have to go now, Uncle Rob, thanks for being honest with me."

"No problem," Rob said. Then he added, "Mike, there's something else."

"What is it?"

"The house. Sometimes I dream about it. I dream that I'm walking through all the rooms and in the dream, I feel like I'm not alone, that there's someone else there, by my shoulder, following me and whispering things into my ear."

"What do they whisper?" Mike asked.

"I have no idea. I also sometimes have a recurring nightmare that I'm walking in the woods behind the house at night. The lake starts to bubble and then dozens of women crawl out of it. They're like zombies, their skin and hair rotting from being under the water. I run to the house and they follow me, crawling over the wall and into the garden. Just as they're about to enter the house, I wake up. What do you think that means?"

"I don't know," Mike told him, although he had a feeling that something had infected his uncle during his two-week stay at the house. Something that had left remnants of itself in Rob's head.

On a whim, Mike called up Rob's travel blog on his phone and selected various dates, looking for the photo Rob had taken of Crow House. It took some time because Rob posted so much. After searching through pictures of Vietnamese rivers and Himalayan mountain ranges, Mike landed on a photo of the Banaue Rice Terraces in the Philippines. It wasn't the picture that interested him so much as a comment below it that read, *Hey, good to see you're back. What happened to you the last couple of weeks?*

Mike clicked on the previous blog entry, which was titled *My House in England* and dated two and a half weeks before the Banaue Rice Terraces picture. The blog entry had a one-line comment from Rob that simply read: *I'm here!* Beneath that was a photograph of Crow House brooding in a shroud of mist.

The house looked as if it were waiting for something.

His recent experiences of Crow House told him that maybe the house *was* waiting for something as it sat in the mist, abandoned and alone. It was waiting for someone to enter the space between its walls and become part of a tragedy that had played out over many years.

Uncle Rob had obviously escaped the house unscathed except for some memory loss, which made Mike think that Rob hadn't been *right* in some way, as far as the house was concerned. He'd been allowed to leave unharmed but a seed had been planted into his mind that would later blossom when Mike's family needed a place to stay.

It had been Rob who'd suggested Mike move his family into the house and it had been Rob who'd suggested July 25th because, in some way, the house had reached into his mind and put the seed of that idea there. Maybe it had happened during the two weeks Rob was at the house or maybe it had been later, when Rob was in the Philippines, dreaming that someone in the house was whispering into his ear.

Either way, Rob's visit to Crow House had set the stage for Mike and his family to move there just as the Gule of August was approaching.

He was about to shut off his phone when he noticed something in the picture that made him look closer. It was no more than a shadow, barely visible in the mist-shrouded trees, but something about it didn't look right. He zoomed in on that area and felt his blood run cold.

It wasn't the shadow of a tree or a trick of the light. It was a man-shaped creature that seemed to be formed of shadow. And within the darkness of its featureless face shone two circles that looked like eyes.

Mike zoomed further onto the face until the picture became grainy and pixelated.

But despite the graininess and distortion, he could tell that those two glowing eyes were looking directly at him.

25

SALT AND FLAME

By the time Mike reached the road that led to Crow House, the sun had long sunk below the horizon and darkness had crept over the woods. The Sportage's headlights cut through the night, illuminating a small section of the road and surrounding trees. The glowing dashboard clock said it was 10:45. Just over an hour to midnight.

He was surprised to find the house in darkness as he approached. It was a barely more than a dark silhouette against the night sky, its only visible features the unlit windows which reflected the moonlight. To Mike, those windows seemed like glowing eyes that stared down at him with an all-seeing gaze as he parked the car by the gate.

He got out quickly and pushed through the gate. He fumbled his key into the front door and opened it onto a hallway hidden in darkness.

He turned on the light and called out, "Terri? Jen?"

His voice echoed hollowly off the walls but there was no reply. The house felt empty.

Mike went into every room on the ground floor and turned on all the lights. They glowed weakly, throwing his shadow faintly onto the walls as he moved through the house.

When he stood in the hallway once more, he directed his gaze upstairs. The landing light was on—because the switch was down here and Mike had flicked it—but the rooms up there lay in darkness.

Where the hell were Terri and Jen? It didn't make sense that they'd leave the house. He ascended the stairs and went to Jen's room, throwing open the door and switching on the light. There was no sign of his daughter.

He turned away from the empty room and opened every door. When he was done, every door—apart from Terri's locked studio door—revealed an empty room. On the slim chance that Terri was in the studio, Mike knocked on the door and said, "Terri, are you in there?"

There was no reply.

Terri and Jen weren't in the house, which meant they had to be in the woods. Something had drawn them there. If Jen was truly possessed, then he could understand why she'd go to the woods but what about Terri? Had Jen somehow convinced her to go there? Mike found that hard to believe; Terri hated the woods and in her current mood, no one could convince her to do anything.

He strode down to the cellar to retrieve the *Daemones Mortum*. When he had the book clutched in his hand, he stood over Jonathan Cain's unmarked grave and swore an oath to avenge the dead man's family.

"I'm going to end this," he said, looking down at the dirt beneath his feet. "That thing in the woods won't take anyone else ever again. It won't tear another family apart."

With that, he left the cellar, taking the box of matches from beside the furnace and grabbing the torch from the top step as he went. When he was back on ground level, he went out to the Sportage and retrieved the bags of salt from the back seat before walking through the house once again and exiting via the back door.

With the book and the bags of salt bundled under one arm, he switched on the torch and used his free hand to swing the beam over the back garden. The gate was open.

Mike went through the opening to the lakeshore and aimed the torch at the edge of the woods. Everything was quiet, with no sign of life.

A rustling in the bushes startled him and he stepped back, dropping the torch, book, and salt. As the torchlight danced wildly before his eyes before coming to rest on the grass, Mike realised he'd come out here into the night with no weapon—except the *Daemones Mortum*—and that oversight might be his downfall.

A dark figure emerged from the bush and said, "Mike, it's me."

Mike didn't recognize the voice or the shape of the man in front of him. "Who?"

The figure bent down slowly and picked up the torch. "Eric Maxwell." He held the light beneath his chin so Mike could see his face. The angle of the beam cast deep shadows over Eric's eye sockets, making him look ghoulish.

"What are you doing here?" Mike whispered.

"I've been watching the house. You told me you weren't going to leave, so I thought I'd stick around to see if you needed my help."

"You could have just knocked on the door instead of skulking out here in the bushes."

"The house looked empty, there were no lights on. Then I saw someone come out of the back door and go into the woods."

"Who was it?"

"I don't know, I couldn't see clearly enough. Look, I've got this." He reached into his jacket pocket and brought out a small object, shining the light on it so Mike could see it clearly.

"A gun?" Mike said when he saw the revolver in Eric's hand.

Eric nodded gravely. "I don't know if it'll work on a demon but I'm willing to give it a shot. It won't bring Simon or his family back but maybe I can avenge them in some way."

"I've got this," Mike told him, picking up the *Daemones Mortum*. Shine the light over here."

Eric shone the light on the book and let out a low whistle. "You found the *Daemones Mortum*. Where was it?"

"In the house," Mike said. "It was burred in the cellar." He didn't feel like mentioning that the book had been buried with its previous owner.

"We can banish the demon," Eric said.

Mike nodded. "Yeah, that's the idea."

"What do we have to do?"

"Only one of us can do it," Mike said. "The talisman has to be worn by the banisher, to protect them from the power of the spell."

"Hand it over," Eric said, holding out his hand. "I'll do it. You can find your wife and daughter and get out of here."

"You sure?"

Eric nodded. "Yeah, I'm sure. I've got nothing to lose if it all goes wrong. The demon has already taken everything I ever cared about. It might end up getting me as well but I'm not going down without a fight. I reckon there are worse ways to go than getting killed while trying to avenge the deaths of your loved ones."

"All right," Mike said, slipping the talisman from his neck and giving it to Eric. "We have to build a fire in the woods. And there are words you have to recite." He opened the book to the appropriate page and showed Eric the spell.

"What are those blank spaces?" Eric asked, frowning at the strange language.

"That's where you have to say the demon's name. Its name is Gethsemiel."

"Gethsemiel," Eric repeated. "Okay, I can remember that."

They picked up the bags of salt and made their way to the woods. Everything was much darker beneath the trees because the canopy of foliage blocked out most of the moonlight. Again, Mike got the eerie feeling that faces were peeking at him from behind the trees.

"You feel that?" Eric asked.

"Feel what?"

"Like we're being watched."

"Yeah."

They found a small clearing and Eric said, "This looks like a good place."

Mike looked at the surrounding area. There was no breeze tonight and without any breeze rustling through the leaves, the woods were eerily quiet. The clearing was close to the rocky promontory that jutted out over the water. Beyond the rock, the lake was smooth as glass, reflecting the moon and stars on its mirror-like surface.

Dropping the salt he was carrying and laying the *Daemones Mortum* on top of the bags along with the matches, Mike said, "I'll gather some firewood."

As he began searching the area for suitable sticks and branches, he was reminded of performing this same act recently with Chris. He'd been telling his son not to be afraid of the woods. That moment seemed like a lifetime ago.

When he returned to the centre of the clearing, Eric was already building a fire, stacking larger branches over thinner sticks and using dead leaves and pieces of bark for kindling.

"Looks like you've done this a few times

before," Mike said, dropping his firewood at Eric's feet.

"Boy Scouts," Eric said. He surveyed his handiwork and, seemingly satisfied, struck a match and touched it to the kindling. The flame caught and the dry leaves and bark began to crackle and smoke.

"You got everything covered here?" Mike asked, anxious to find Terri and Jen.

Eric nodded and held up a small stick. "I've got this to draw those weird symbols in the air and the words in the book should do the rest. You should go find your wife and daughter now and get them the hell out of here."

"I will," Mike said, shaking Eric's hand. "Thank you and…be safe." He didn't know what else to say. What was the correct farewell when someone was about to cast a spell to banish a demon?

"You too," Eric said, "and don't worry about me. I'll get the salt circle drawn and then I just need to wait until midnight."

Mike checked the time on his phone. Twenty minutes left before the Gule of August began. He didn't have long to find Jen and Terri. He supposed a good place to start might be the small ramshackle house that sat among the trees. At least if he started at the house and worked out from there, his search would be more structured. Otherwise, he'd be wandering aimlessly and tonight of all nights, he didn't want to be blindly stumbling around in the woods.

Leaving the clearing and making his way through the trees, he again felt that unseen eyes were watching him from the darkness beyond the reach of his torchlight. He cast a glance over his shoulder to see if anyone was behind him but all he saw was Eric in the distance, illuminated by the fire, pouring salt from the bags to form a circle of protection.

He wondered if the demon knew they were here, in its territory, preparing to destroy it. Surely if it knew, it would try to stop them.

Maybe it's too busy preparing to take its victims.

Don't think like that. Those victims are your wife and child.

That thought increased his pace.

When the house came into view, it was veiled in darkness. There was no candle burning in the window, no signs of life at all. Even though the house stood in darkness, Mike went inside anyway just to be sure there was no one there. He cast the torch's beam around the rooms but the place was empty. So where did he go from here? The woods were immense and if the demon had a lair somewhere, Mike had no idea where it was.

He wondered if the lake might be a good place to start. After all, that was where the witches had been drowned and those witches had become the demon's sacrifices.

He left the house and aimed the torch at the big oak tree where he'd seen Sam's body. The tree looked normal, just as it had when he'd shown it to Battle.

When he turned his attention back in the direction of the lake, Mike started as the light picked up a figure standing among the trees.

His heart leaped in his chest and he jumped back slightly, wondering if the demon had come to stop him after all. Maybe Eric was already dead, lying by the blazing fire with his stomach ripped open and guts spilling onto the ground, and now it was Mike's turn.

Then he came to the realisation that the figure was no demon. It was Jonathan Cain, or his ghost at least.

Steadying his breathing, Mike approached Cain. "We're trying to destroy it," he told the ghost. "I need to find my wife and daughter so I can save them."

Cain raised one arm and pointed into the dark woods.

Sudden hope flared in Mike. "Do you know where they are?"

Cain nodded slowly and then turned and

began walking in the direction he'd been pointing.

Mike followed, checking the time on his phone.

The glowing digits read *00:00.*

The Gule of August had arrived.

26

GULE OF AUGUST

Mike followed the ghost of Jonathan Cain through the woods, unsure of where he was going but trusting Cain to show him where Terri and Jen were. He didn't have much time now; midnight had arrived and Eric would be casting the banishment spell. The power of that spell would destroy anyone who wasn't wearing a talisman of protection and Mike had no idea how far he had to get his family away from here to keep them from being affected by that power.

Cain stopped suddenly and pointed at a clearing that was not unlike the one where Mike and Eric had built the fire. There was no fire here, though. Instead, a crude stone altar carved with geometrical symbols Mike didn't recognise occupied the centre of the clearing.

As he approached the structure, he heard a low sobbing and increased his pace when he recognised the sound as one he'd heard many times before. It was the sound Jen had made when, at five years old, she'd fallen off her bike and scraped her knees on the pavement. It was the same sob she'd emitted when she was eight and her pet hamster, Mr Snuggles, had died. And it was the same anguished sound she'd made when her grandmother— Mike's mother Sylvia—had finally succumbed to lung cancer.

His daughter was here somewhere and she was in pain.

Mike rushed to the altar and found Jen lying on the other side of it, curled into the fetal position, legs drawn up to her chest. Her hair covered her face and for a sickly moment, Mike was reminded of Eliza Cain in his dream vision, her face carved with a pentagram.

"Jen," he said, crouching next to her and touching her shoulder.

She looked up at him with one red-rimmed eye, her face wrought in total anguish. Her hair fell away from her face and Mike breathed a sigh of relief. His daughter was unmarked.

"Dad," she said between sobs, "I don't know what's happening. I didn't want to come here but she made me."

"Who?" he asked, taking her into his arms. "Who made you?"

"Eliza," she said coldly. "She...got inside me somehow. She's a ghost or something, I don't know. She made me come here because she wants me to be sacrificed to the demon."

"Gethsemiel," Mike said.

"He Who Roams the Woods," Jen whispered.

"We're getting out of here." Mike pulled her to her feet. "Where's your mother?"

Jen frowned, confused. "Isn't she at the house?"

Mike shook his head. "I checked every room except her studio."

"Maybe she's in there. She's always in there."

Mike hoped his daughter was right. If Terri was somewhere out here in the woods, there was no way he'd find her. At least if he got Jen back to the house, he could check the studio before driving out of here.

And if Terri isn't there? Are you still going to drive away?

He didn't know the answer to that question, didn't want to think about it at the moment. Right now, he had to focus on getting Jen to safety. "Come on," he said, "let's go."

They left the clearing and made their way through the trees. Mike wasn't sure of the exact direction they should go—Jonathan Cain's ghost seemed to have disappeared—but he knew that if he kept the lake in view and didn't stray too far away from it, they'd eventually reach Crow House.

He just prayed they got there before Eric completed the banishing spell.

27

FROM BENEATH

Eric was having trouble reading the words from the *Daemones Mortum*. He'd started off okay—or at least he'd thought so—but as the spell went on, the strange words seemed to swim on the page before him. Not only that, the geometric symbols he was supposed to draw in the air before him with the stick were complex and he was sure he was getting them wrong.

He'd told Mike Wilson, in a moment of bravado, that if the demon got him, at least he'd go down fighting but now that he was trying to cast the spell and getting it all wrong, he realised that it was entirely his responsibility to banish Gethsemiel. If he failed now, the demon would keep on destroying the lives of good folk.

That was a huge responsibility to shoulder and Eric was sure he'd already messed up the spell enough that it wasn't going to work. Maybe he should cut and run, help Mike get his family out of here, and live to fight another day.

The only thing that gave him a glimmer of hope was the fact that *something* was happening as he recited the words from the *Daemones Mortum*. It felt as if the air within the circle had become charged with electricity, a power that seemed to be building. Eric could feel it tingling along the skin on his arms and face. The hairs on the back of his neck stood to static attention.

He only hoped that this building charge of energy meant he was casting the banishment correctly, despite his doubts. The book gave no indication of what would happen once the spell was in motion, other than warning that it would destroy anyone not wearing the talisman.

So Eric continued reciting the words from the book and added the demon's name, Gethsemiel, where the blank spaces indicated to do so. He clumsily attempted to inscribe the complex geometrical shapes in the air and hoped that Mike had found his wife and daughter and escaped the area.

Simon, Wendy, and Claire had met a tragic

end but perhaps it wasn't too late for the Wilson family.

Just as he was about to attempt yet another shape with his stick, a noise from the lake startled Eric. He turned his head in that direction, still trying to draw the pattern in the air because he was afraid to halt the spell in the middle of casting it. Who knew what might happen if he stopped?

But when he saw what was happening at the lake, he felt a cold shiver of fear run through his body. The water, which had been as smooth as a sheet of glass earlier, was bubbling and frothing. As Eric watched, a hand appeared, clawing at the earth at the lake's edge, then another, and another. Each hand, and the arm attached to it, looked grey and mottled, the flesh ragged and torn.

And then the heads appeared out of the frothing water, bloated female heads with long white hair and mouths that grinned toothless smiles. The bloated, rotten faces held milky eyes that looked as if they shouldn't be able to see but which were clearly fixed on Eric.

The words of the spell faltered in his throat as dozens of long-limbed, rotting women crawled out of the lake and scuttled through the undergrowth towards him.

"No," he cried, reaching for the revolver in

his waistband and pulling it free. The spell was ruined. He knew that now. He also knew that there was no way he could use the gun to get out of this situation; it only held six bullets yet there were at least thirty or forty of these undead women rushing at him from the depths of the lake.

For one foolish moment, he thought the salt circle might save him, that the rotting witches —for that was what he was sure they were, the remains of the witches who had been drowned her centuries ago—might not be able to cross the barrier.

But the witches scuttled over the salt with impunity, scattering it in all directions. The circle was broken.

Eric screamed as the first hands grabbed at him and he was pulled off his feet. The hands felt slimy and there was a stench of rotten fish, weed, and putrid flesh in the air. He gagged on it, feeling it fill his nostril and lungs.

The witches dragged him back the way they had come, towards the lake. Eric screamed again when he realised they meant to drown him. His mind raced with fear. If they drowned him, as they had been drowned hundreds of years ago, would he simply die or would something worse happen to him? He might become one of them, festering in the depths of the lake until the next Gule of August, when he would crawl out of the lake, rotten and bloated.

He saw only one way to escape a fate worse than death. He brought the muzzle of the revolver up and pressed it against his temple.

28

IMAGES AND WORDS

When Mike heard the single gunshot ring out, he and Jen were almost at Crow House. Jen seemed stronger now, both physically and in spirit, moving purposefully toward the gate with a steely look in her eyes. The farther she'd come from the ancient altar in the woods, the more her old self had returned.

The sound of the shot stopped Mike in his tracks. He turned and looked at the area where he and Eric had built the fire. He could see the flames dimly, flickering in the distance through the trees.

Another sound followed the shot, a low *wump* that sounded like a wet paper bag exploding. Then Mike saw something coming toward him through the trees: an expanding ring of spectral blue light that seemed to radiate from the area where the fire still burned. The trees trembled as the light passed through them. The leaves on the ground were blown into the air as if being stirred by a hurricane.

Some sort of energy had been released. Was this the power of the spell, the energy the book warned about?

"Jen, get behind the wall!" Mike shouted, following his daughter through the gate and crouching next to her, pressing himself against to the stone wall.

He heard the ring of energy passing through the trees, rustling them as it got closer to the house. Then the wall trembled and the bushes in the garden shook. The blue light passed over Mike and Jen and radiated across the garden and through the house. The walls shuddered and the windowpanes rattled but Crow House remained steadfast against the mysterious blue light.

"What was that?" Jen asked, getting to her feet.

"I think it was the energy of the spell. Or at least some of the energy. I think it lost most of its power because Eric didn't finish casting it." Whatever had happened in the woods, the gunshot had seemed final and the dissipating energy suggested that the spell had failed.

"We have to get out of here," Mike said. "We tried to banish the demon and failed and now it's going to be as mad as hell."

As he spoke the words, he heard something else rustling through the undergrowth toward the house. It wasn't a band of energy this time, though. As he peered into the darkness, Mike saw human shapes crawling through the woods at an alarming speed.

"We should get in the house," Jen said, her gaze fixed on the figures, which Mike could now see were white-haired women with mottled skin and water-bloated features.

He ushered Jen in through the back door and followed her inside, locking the door behind him.

"The car," he said. "We need to get to the car."

"What about Mum?"

"I'll find her. Here, take these." He handed her the keys to the Sportage. "If I don't come out soon, drive to the village. Wait there for a while. If I still don't appear, drive to Matlock. Your brother's there in the Traveller's Inn. The address is in the SatNav."

"Dad, you're scaring me. Of course you'll come out. We'll go to the Traveller's Inn together. You, me, and Mum."

Mike could tell that even as she said the

words, she was trying to convince herself and not really believing what she was saying.

"Of course," he said, even though he didn't believe it himself. Everything was not going to be all right. If Terri was in her studio, why hadn't she come out when he'd knocked on the door and called her name earlier?

A loud *thump* sounded as something heavy hit the back door. Then another. And another. Mottled grey hands appeared at the kitchen windows, banging on the glass. The hideous faces of the women stared into the house, milky white eyes seeking prey.

"The witches," Jen said.

"Go!" Mike shouted at Jen, pushing her along the hallway and out the front door. He vaulted up the stairs to Terri's studio and was surprised, when he got to the landing, to find the door open.

The studio was in darkness. Mike flicked the switch. As the bulb came to life and illuminated the room, Mike stepped back in shock.

Terri had set up her easel in the centre of the space, with her brushes, paints, and sketchbook on a table that ran along the wall. A large canvas sat on the easel but Mike couldn't see what had been painted on it because it was covered with a blanket. What Mike *could* see, though, and what had shocked him were the words Terri had painted on the walls in black paint. The same two words, repeated over and over on every wall.

Mary Cain.

The name of Jonathan Cain's dead wife had been painted with delicate brushstrokes in some places and with clumsy, slashing strokes in others.

As Mike let his eyes roam the room, they came to rest on something on the ceiling. Terri had something there, in simple black lines, above her easel. As Mike peered closer, he could see that the image was that of a woman's face. Half of the face was covered by the woman's long hair and she looked down from the ceiling with a single, staring eye.

Mike had no idea why Terri had painted the face on the ceiling like that but the way it stared down at him creeped him out. He was almost afraid to pull back the blanket that covered the easel but knew he had to see what Terri had spent all her time painting since they'd come to Crow House.

He grabbed one corner of the blanket and tossed it aside, uncovering the painting. He wasn't sure what he'd expected to see painted on the canvas—perhaps another portrait of the woman on the ceiling or simply the words *Mary Cain,* like those on the walls—but he hadn't expected a depiction of the woods in the moonlight.

The painting included the house's rear wall and gate and part of the lake and Mike guessed from the way the trees were painted from a slightly elevated viewpoint that Terri had viewed the scene from the window in this room.

There seemed to be nothing remarkable about the picture—it certainly wasn't as disturbing as the face on the ceiling or the name repeated over the walls—until Mike took a closer look at the shadows beneath the trees. One of them didn't seem quite right. And as he inspected it, he realised that it wasn't a shadow at all but a tall, dark figure with two shiny eyes. It looked exactly like the figure on the photo Uncle Rob had taken when he'd arrived at Crow House.

Gethsemiel.

A loud crash from downstairs pulled his attention from the painting. The witches had broken through the back door and were inside the house. He could hear their fingernails clattering over the floor tiles as they sought him out.

He had to get out of here. Jen was sitting out front in the Sportage and Mike had no idea how long it would be before the witches went out there and tried to get into the car. Some of them might be out there already.

He rushed down the stairs and got to the hallway just as a throng of witches scuttled out of the kitchen toward him. They grabbed for his legs and ankles, their wet hands sliding over his jeans.

Mike kicked at them and flung the front door open. He looked over at the Sportage and let out a relieved breath when he saw that there were no witches around the car. Jen was sitting in the driver's seat and she had the engine running. She looked at him with wide eyes and gestured for him to get in the vehicle.

Mike ran over and got in the passenger side. The hideously-bloated women were crawling out of Crow House now, making their way to the vehicle with murderous intent in their moon-white eyes.

"Drive," Mike said.

Jen already had the car in gear and she released the handbrake before flooring the accelerator. The Sportage lurched forward and picked up speed, its headlights lighting up the road ahead.

"Where's Mum?" Jen asked hesitantly.

"I couldn't find her. She wasn't in the house." He turned in his seat to look out of the back window. The horde of witches had seemingly disappeared.

As he turned to face front again, he saw a pale figure standing in the middle of the road, illuminated in the car's headlights. Jen screamed and spun the steering wheel to the left to avoid hitting the figure.

The car turned violently and Mike saw nothing but trees in the headlights. For a split second, he was sure he and Jen were going to die here. At the speed they were moving, a head-on collision with a tree would surely be fatal.

But Jen reacted quickly, turning the wheel to the right to correct their course. The Sportage skidded. As the front of the car turned back toward the road, the rear end fishtailed into the grass. Mike heard a loud *crash* and felt a jolt as the back of the vehicle hit a tree. The rear window shattered.

Jen floored the accelerator and the car shot back onto the road, skidding crazily when Jen hit the brakes and brought the Sportage to a stop.

"What are you doing?" Mike said. "Why are we stopping?"

"That was Mum!" Leaving the car idling, Jen opened her door and got out.

"Jen, no!" Mike shouted but his daughter was already running back along the road.

He threw open his door and jumped out, calling after Jen again. She ignored him and continued running toward the pale figure, which Mike now recognised as his wife.

Terri was dressed in one of her nightgowns —a white diaphanous affair that Mike had bought her a few years ago for her birthday or Valentine's Day, he couldn't remember which— and in her left hand, she held a kitchen knife. Her hair hung over one side of her face, exactly like the woman's hair in the portrait on the studio ceiling. She stood stock still, staring at Jen with her one visible eye. Illuminated by the red rear lights of the Sportage, she looked demonic.

"Jen, stop!" Mike shouted.

Jen did so, but Mike was sure it wasn't because she was heeding his words. Her hand went to her mouth and she screamed, shaking her head as if denial of something. She turned away from her mother and ran into Mike's arms, terrified. "Dad, look at her face."

Mike held his daughter tightly and turned to Terri. His wife looked at him dispassionately and used the tip of the kitchen knife to brush her hair back from her face. Mike already knew what he was going to see but the sight of the pentagram carved into Terri's flesh, stretching from her forehead all the way down to her lower cheek, still shocked him.

"It made me do it," Terri said, her voice tinged with a hint of despair.

"Terri, come with us," Mike said. "We can leave here."

She shook her head. "I can't."

She pointed to the side of the road. Mike looked in that direction and took an involuntary step backwards when he saw the tall shadowy figure with shining eyes standing among the trees. He instinctively held Jen closer.

The demon stared at Mike for a moment and then turned its attention to Terri. She began to walk towards it.

"Terri, stop!" Mike shouted.

Ignoring him, his wife took two more steps towards the edge of the road.

"Jen, get in the car," Mike said, pushing his daughter towards the Sportage. He waited until she was inside the vehicle and then rushed over to Terri, intent on stopping her. He'd drag her to the car if he had to.

When he reached her, she was already in the trees. Mike stepped forward to grab her arm but as he did so, the ground beneath his feet erupted and he was thrown onto his back. The air exploded from his lungs and he watched helplessly as Terri continued to walk away into the darkness and a deep hole had formed in the ground.

As he struggled to his feet, he felt a force like a thousand hands pulling him towards the makeshift grave. He lost his footing and the unseen hands dragged him through the undergrowth toward the hole.

He cried out and tried to scramble back across the grass to the road before he could be buried alive. But he was being dragged to his doom. He clawed at the ground and held onto half-sunken tree roots but the force pulling him to the grave was irresistible.

A hand appeared in his vision, reaching down in front of his face from the direction of the road. Mike looked up and saw Jonathan Cain standing there. Cain looked at Mike with an expression of sincerity that seemed to say, "Trust me."

Mike reached for the proffered hand and took it. Cain's fingers curled around Mike's and then Mike felt himself being dragged to the road. Once he was away from the grass and kneeling on the road itself, the force that had been pulling him towards the hole dissipated.

Mike stood up and faced the ghost of Jonathan Cain. "Thank you," he said, "but I have to and get my wife back." He made a move to the trees but Cain grabbed him by the shoulders and turned him around so he was facing the Sportage.

Shaking off the grip, Mike faced Cain again and said, "My wife. I have to save her."

Cain shook his head gently and pointed at the car.

Mike understood what the ghost was trying to tell him. Cain had lost his wife *and* daughter to the demon. It was too late for Terri but Mike still had a chance to save Jen. Cain obviously wanted Mike to avoid the complete tragedy he himself had experienced a century ago.

The realisation that he would never see his wife again struck Mike like a punch to the gut. How would Chris—easily the most sensitive of their two children—be affected by having to go through life without a mother? How would Jen cope with losing her mother on top of everything else she'd experienced lately?

Hot tears burned his eyes and Mike wiped them away, turning to the car. He had to get Jen out of here; for all he knew, the demon would come back here to take her, just as it had taken Terri.

He slid into the passenger seat and said, "We need to go, Jen."

She was crying, gripping the wheel so

tightly that her knuckles were white. "You couldn't save her," she said.

"No," Mike said grimly. "If it wasn't for Jonathan Cain, I'd be dead too."

She looked at him, frowning. "What do you mean?"

"Jonathan Cain," he said, turning in his seat and pointing at Cain, who was standing in the middle of the road watching the car. "He's right there."

Jen shook her head. "There's no one there, Dad."

Mike turned to face front again and said, "Just drive. Let's put as much road between us and this place as we can."

She put the Sportage in gear and set off along the road, away from Crow House. Mike turned in his seat once again and watched Jonathan Cain through the jagged hole where the rear window had once been. Cain stood in the middle of the road and watched them go, giving Mike a slight nod.

Mike nodded back. Without Cain, Chris and Jen would probably be dead, along with their mother.

The ghost had saved his family.

29

SEEING THE UNSEEN

August 2ND

DCI Battle stood by the front gate of Crow House while he waited for the forensic team to finish their job. The team had been here for hours, scouring the house with swabs and vacuums, meticulously collecting evidence and sealing it in clear plastic bags that would be opened at the lab and have their contents analysed by a mass spectrometer.

Battle was here not because he was interested in the collection of microscopic evidence but because he wanted to get a feel for the place.

Mike Wilson had called him in the early hours of yesterday morning, telling Battle that he was holed up at the Traveller's Inn in Matlock and that his wife, Terri, was dead.

Battle had rung DS Lyons, waking her up in the process, and told her to prepare an interview room at the Matlock police station, saying he would meet her there after he'd picked up Mike Wilson. Then he'd gone to the Traveller's Inn, ushered Wilson into his Range Rover and taken him to the station for questioning while a female detective—DS Waters—and a male social worker, whose name Battle didn't know, stayed with the children.

Mike Wilson had told a story that had seemed, to Battle, to be fairly fantastic. Mike had claimed that his wife, Terri, had become mentally disturbed and wandered away into the woods. Mike had said that although he hadn't seen his wife die (and the police team searching the woods hadn't found a body yet), he was certain that she was, indeed, dead. That struck Battle as odd. How could Mike be so sure his wife was dead if he hadn't witnessed her death himself? She might be wandering around in the trees, lost and confused, for all her husband knew.

The Wilson children had been interviewed by DS Waters at the hotel but the statements they'd given her didn't shed any light on what had actually happened here yesterday. Jen

Wilson had claimed memory loss and Chris had said he'd been ensconced in the hotel room during the night in question.

It all seemed a bit too convenient to Battle. With no witnesses, no evidence, and no statements that amounted to anything concrete, the truth could be far removed from Mike Wilson's story.

DS Lyons came out of the house, followed by a dozen forensic scientists in white protective suits. "They're all done, guv," she said.

Peterson, who was in charge of the forensic team, came out of the house after his team and took off his mask.

"Anything?" Battle asked.

Peterson shrugged. "Difficult to tell at first blush. We've collected a lot of material from the floors and other surfaces. There's nothing obvious like blood spray on the kitchen wall or anything like that, if that's what you mean."

"That would have made my job a hell of a lot easier," Battle observed.

"Looks like someone's bashed the back door down," Peterson said. "And we did discover one strange thing: there's water on the kitchen floor, leading into the hall and out here. Looks like there are particles of human flesh in it."

Battle perked up.

"Before you get your hopes up," Peterson

said, "the flesh is putrid. It certainly doesn't belong to the Wilson woman unless she's been dead for a good few years."

"Old dead flesh," Battle mused, "What does that mean?"

"I was hoping you'd know," Peterson said, "because I have no bloody idea." He turned his attention to the forensic vans and shouted at his team. "Come on, let's get this stuff loaded and down to the lab." Then he gestured at Crow House and said to Battle, "The house is all yours. Good luck."

"Thanks," Battle said, wondering why he'd gotten himself involved in this case. Since the Maxwell case in the 70s, he'd repeatedly sworn to himself that he'd stay away from Crow House. Too much of what happened here seemed to defy the science and logic on which a good police investigation was based. But he didn't seem able to keep away. The house had crawled under his skin when he'd first come here all those years ago and now it was like an itch he had to scratch.

He went inside, closely followed by DS Lyons, and stood in the hallway for a moment, imagining what the scene would have looked like last night, in the dark. "Probably bloody depressing," he muttered to himself.

"What's that, guv?" Lyons asked.

"I was just thinking that living here could be enough to drive anyone mad. There's an atmosphere here. It's oppressive. Can you feel it?"

She shrugged. "No."

"These walls have seen a lot of tragedy," he told her. "Sometimes that kind of thing lingers."

"You mean ghosts?" She arched a quizzical eyebrow. Battle knew Lyons was a skeptic regarding most things, and that was usually a good trait for a detective to possess, but he tended to think that an open mind was advantageous at times.

"I'm not sure what I mean," he said. "But over the years, a lot of bad things have happened in this house and the surrounding area. It has to be more than just coincidence."

"Maybe the house attracts bad people," she said. "Bad people do bad things."

"You think Simon Maxwell was a bad person?"

"That case was before my time, guv."

He sighed, feeling suddenly old. "Yes, I suppose it was. Mike Wilson, then. We hardly knew him but did he seem like a murderer to you?"

She considered that for a moment before answering, "I guess not, but he was definitely unhinged in some way."

He held up a finger and said, "Consider this: what if it was the house that made him that way?"

Before Lyons had a chance to answer, DS Kirk—a young detective Battle had sent out to the woods with the search team—came in through the back door. "You're going to want to see this, guv."

"All right, lead the way," Battle told him.

Kirk led them out into the garden and through the back gate. As they skirted the lake, Battle could hear dogs barking in the woods.

"The cadaver dogs found something?" he asked Kirk.

"Not exactly, guv. The dogs have been going nuts all day, as if they can smell cadavers everywhere. It's like someone dragged a dozen dead bodies all around the woods. The dog handlers can't make head nor tail of it."

"So what *have* you found?"

"I don't know how to explain it," Kirk said.

Battle looked at Lyons and arched an eyebrow. She returned the gesture with a slight shrug.

"Come on, lad, spit it out," Battle told Kirk, "What is it?"

"I've been in these woods probably a hundred times," Kirk said as they walked beneath the trees. "I know this area like the back of my hand, or at least I thought I did. Yet I've never seen or heard of what we found this morning. But it's been there for a long time, it has to have been."

"You're rambling," Battle told him.

"Sorry, guv. It isn't far. That's what makes no sense. It isn't far at all from the house or the lake yet no one on the search team has ever seen it before, and some of them have been hiking in these woods all their lives."

"For God's sake," Battle said, frustrated now, "what is it, lad?"

"It's this," Kirk said, leading them into a clearing. A number of police officers were gathered around something that looked like a huge stone altar, at least ten feet long and standing five feet high. The officers were inspecting it with questioning expressions on their faces. Battle felt as confused as they looked. He'd been in this part of the woods plenty of times—they were no more than fifty yards from the lake and barely more than a stone's throw from Crow House—yet he'd never seen this clearing before, or the stone altar at its centre.

He frowned, doubting his own memory for the first time in his life. In the distance, the cadaver dogs still barked crazily.

"We're going to need to get forensics out

here, sir," one of the officers said, approaching Battle. "There's blood on the stone and on the ground surrounding it. And there's a trail of blood that seems to lead from the altar to the lake."

"Kirk, get hold of Peterson," Battle said. "Tell him his job isn't done yet." He turned to the officer, whose name he now remembered was Collier, and said, in a low voice, "What is this place?"

"Looks like an ancient place of worship of some kind, sir. There are runes carved into the altar."

"Yes, yes, I can see that. I mean how long has it been here?"

Collier shrugged. " I don't know, sir. Maybe five thousand years?"

"Five thousand years," Battle repeated.

"That's about how old Stonehenge is, sir."

"So this thing has been sitting here in the woods for thousands of years and no one has ever come across it before?"

"Seems that way, sir."

Battle turned to Lyons. "What do you make of it?"

"I don't know, guv," she said, stepping closer to the altar. "I can't explain it. I've been in this area a few times before but I've never seen this clearing or the altar."

Battle looked around the clearing, at the carved stone altar, and at the blood on the ground. "So why are we seeing it now?"

"No idea, guv."

The idea that they were being allowed to see what had previously been hidden gave Battle the chills. He turned away from the altar and left the clearing, Lyons close behind.

As he strode back to the house, Battle mulled over the appearance of the altar. The police had searched this particular stretch of woods many times over the years but no one had ever seen the altar. There wasn't a single mention of it on any report Battle had ever read.

"Something prevented us from seeing that place," he told Lyons. "Or if we *did* see it, something made us forget."

"But we can see it now," Lyons said.

"That's what worries me."

"I'm not sure what you mean, guv."

"It's as if whatever was hiding the altar isn't bothered anymore. Something's changed. If it was hiding the altar for so long, why would it stop now?"

Lyons shrugged. "Maybe it's moved on."

"Moved on," Battle repeated, muttering the words to himself. He remembered something that Simon Maxwell had told him in the 70s while being questioned about the murder of his wife and child. At the time, the words had seemed insignificant but now, they held a relevance that hit Battle in the gut like a physical punch.

"We need to get to the Travellers Inn," he told Lyons as he broke into a run. "And get hold of Dispatch. Tell them to send every available officer to the hotel."

"What is it, guv?" she asked, sprinting along beside him. "What's wrong?"

"Simon Maxwell told me that he murdered his wife and daughter because he was trying to stop the evil from spreading. He said that if he hadn't done it, they'd have killed him and then made their way to the village. To civilisation, he said. I think the demon's become bloody bored waiting out here for the occasional hiker to kill. It just needed the right family to come along so it could make its escape."

"The Maxwells?"

"It tried to use the Maxwells but that didn't work because Simon killed Wendy and Claire." He ran through the gate and through the house to where his Land Rover was parked out front. He scrambled into the driver's seat.

"It waited all these years for a family like the Wilsons to arrive at Crow House," he told Lyons as she got into the passenger seat. "Now it's out there, where it wants to be, away from these lonely woods and in the town, where there are more people."

"I'm not sure I follow, guv."

"The demon used the girl," he said as he started the engine. "It's inside Jen Wilson."

30

THE ROOM

The Travellers Inn car park was packed with police vehicles and ambulances when Battle sped into the car park. He slammed on the brakes, jumped out of the Land Rover and grabbed the nearest constable. "What happened?"

"Not exactly sure, sir. We've got two bodies inside."

Battle pushed his way through the throng of uniformed officers, closely followed by DS Lyons, and strode into the building. The hotel receptionist was sitting in one of the chairs in the foyer, giving a tear-laden statement to a female constable. The door to the inner part of the building, which was usually only accessible with a keycard, was wedged open. Battle saw spots of blood on the carpet, leading out into the foyer.

"She came running through here like a wild beast," the receptionist was telling the constable.

Battle went through the open doorway and along the corridor to the room where he'd collected Mike Wilson before taking him to the station. There were streaks of blood on the walls here and Battle feared the worst for DS Waters and the social worker he'd left here with her.

The door to the room was open and a number of officers were milling about in the corridor outside, talking in low voices. As he got closer to the room, Battle could smell the coppery tang of blood in the air. He'd smelled the sickly-sweet odour of death many times before in his career but all he could smell in the hotel hallway was blood, which meant the people in the room had only recently been killed and their bodies had not yet begun to rot.

"What's the situation?" he asked the officer closest to him, a detective named Sims.

"We came here as per your orders, guv. When we got here, the receptionist was trying to call us but she was shaking so much she couldn't dial the number. She told us a teenage girl had run out from this area into the foyer.

Apparently, her hands were covered in blood. We came back here and found this." He indicated the room beyond the open door.

Battle looked inside. DS Waters lay on the floor at the foot of one the of the room's two double beds, her chest and stomach covered in blood and her own internal organs. The social worker was slumped in one corner, his torso in a similar bloody state. The walls were covered with streaks and spatters of blood that stood out like bright crimson slashes against the white paint.

"Where's the boy?"

"Boy, guv?"

"The boy who was here. Chris Wilson. Where is he?" He pushed past the detective and opened the door to the room's bathroom. There was no one in there and, unlike the main part of the room, the walls were pristine.

Lyons went to the wardrobe and opened it. "He's in here, guv."

Battle went over to the wardrobe and crouched down. Chris Wilson was curled up in the corner, his hands over his mouth as he tried not to make any noise to betray his position. Tears ran from his eyes and his chest hitched silently.

"Hey, Chris," Battle said, "I'm going to get you out of here, okay?"

Chris nodded so imperceptibly that Battle might have missed it if he hadn't been paying close attention.

He reached into the wardrobe and put his arms around the boy's back. "Come on, I'm going to carry you." He reasoned that if he carried Chris out of the room, he could keep the boy's face pressed against his shoulder and keep the lad from seeing the horrific sights in the room.

He regretted that decision when he felt how heavy Chris was. As he struggled into an upright position, the boy held tight against him, Battle was grateful when Lyons put her hands under his shoulders and helped him up.

Turning to the door, Battle shot Sims a look of disapproval.

Sims shrugged helplessly. "We only just got here, we didn't know there was a boy in the room."

Ignoring him, Battle carried Chris out of the room and along the corridor to the foyer. Only then did he put the boy down. "We're going to take you to the police station so you can see your dad, Chris. Does that sound okay?"

Chris nodded. His arms hung limply by his sides and his eyes had a faraway look in them. Battle recognised the signs of shock. Once they got outside, he'd get the boy a blanket to keep him warm.

"She looked crazy and she was covered in the blood," the receptionist was saying to the female constable.

"Come on, Chris," Battle said, leading the boy outside.

"She's right," Chris said in words that were barely more than a whisper. "My sister went crazy. She killed those people." He began to cry again.

"We can talk about that another time," Battle told him, "You don't have to think about it right now." But he knew that images of the events that had occurred in the hotel room would be playing over and over in the boy's head. And they'd probably haunt him for the rest of his life.

31

THE GRAVE

Highgate Cemetery, London
August 1st
One Year Later

Mike stood with his hands on his son's shoulders as they both stood in the rain looking down at Terri's grave and the bright bouquet flowers they'd just placed there.

Mike wondered that Chris was thinking about but refrained from asking; the boy's thoughts were his own business. Mike only hoped they were of happier times and not of the final week before Terri's death.

He tried not to think of that time himself but usually found his mind pondering those fateful seven days, wondering if he could have done anything differently and saved his family.

The unwelcome conclusion he always came to was that he *could* have acted differently but he'd been too closed-minded at the time to believe what was happening in front of his own eyes.

The sense of guilt he felt every time he visited Terri's grave was crushing. His wife was gone and it was probably his fault. He'd been so obsessed with the old letters and the damned spell book that he'd had no idea Terri was being influenced by the demon. If he'd been more attentive, he might have seen warning signs.

The police had combed the woods behind Crow House and sent divers into the lake to search for his wife's body but had found nothing other than an altar in a clearing which had apparently been "hidden" by some means. In the interview room, DCI Battle had put forward the theory to Mike that the revelation of the altar meant the demon had moved away from the area.

Considering the events that took place later, in the Travellers Inn, when Jen attacked and killed two people before fleeing the hotel, Mike had to agree.

He gently steered Chris away from the

grave and back to the path that led through the gravestones.

As they walked through the rain towards the cemetery gates, Chris said, "Why didn't she kill me, Dad?"

"Because she's your sister and she loves you." It was a question Chris asked many times and Mike always gave exactly the same answer so that now it was like a mantra between them.

And the answer, Mike hoped, contained at least a grain of truth. He clung to the belief that there had been enough of Jen still left inside her body that she'd spared Chris's life. He didn't want to acknowledge the possibility that she would have ended her brother's life if Chris hadn't crawled inside the wardrobe as soon as the killing had started.

He was sure Chris also thought about that possibility regularly and used the mantra as a means of self-assurance that he'd survived because Jen had cared for him and not simply because he'd hidden. The boy was disturbed to his core and no amount of therapy or grief counseling was ever going to change that.

The rain became a downpour, pounding the cemetery with heavy drops that exploded on the path.

"Come on, Dad, we can shelter under there,"

Chris said, pointing at a large, old oak tree growing among a jumble of gravestones. The stones stood at odd angles, like teeth in a rotting mouth, pushed up by the roots of the tree.

Mike hesitated. The tree reminded him of the oak tree by the little house in the woods, in which Sam Wetherby had been entombed.

But Chris was already running towards it, weaving around the higgledy-piggledy gravestones and splashing through the wet mud and grass.

Mike followed his son, telling himself that there was nothing to fear here. They were in London, miles away from Crow House and the tree that had seemingly swallowed a young man.

When they were both standing beneath the tree's thick limbs, Chris looked up at the grey sky. "How long do you think this will last?"

Assuming the question was about the rain and not something deeper like grief or the pain of loss, Mike said, "I have no idea." He realised the answer was appropriate if Chris had simply been asking the downpour and also if the question had been about deeper, more philosophical, matters.

His phone buzzed and Mike reached into

his pocket for it. "It's probably work," he told Chris. Last year, after the events at Crow House, Mike had received a call from an old work colleague, telling him that a new advertising company had sprung up in London and they were building a sales team. If Mike was interested, there were jobs available. Mike had applied, gone for a series of interviews, and ended up with a team leader job.

Ironically, his old firm had also contacted him and said they were hiring. If Mike wanted his old job back, it was his. Mike had declined. Going back there would be too much like returning to his old life, before Crow House, only this time he wouldn't have Terri or Jen. He didn't want to take a step backwards.

His new job was a step forward and provided the means for him and Chris to live in a little flat in Bromley. They were surviving.

He'd taken today off to visit the grave with Chris but that didn't mean someone from his team wasn't calling him with a question or asking for advice about something.

When he looked at the phone, though, the display told him it wasn't his firm calling.

It was Uncle Rob.

Mike hadn't heard from his uncle in over a year. He'd tried to ring Rob numerous times to tell him what had happened at Crow House but had received no answer to any of his calls. Guessing that Rob had left the Philippines and was now living in a part of the world where there was no phone reception, Mike had eventually given up, assuming Rob would call *him* at some point to ask how his house sitters were doing.

But Rob had never called.

Mike brought the phone to his ear. "Hello?"

Rob's voice was just as Mike remembered it but his uncle sounded sleepy. "Hey, Mike, it's me. Long time no hear."

"Rob, where have you been? I tried to call you." Mike felt a sudden surge of emotion as he realised he was going to have to tell his uncle that Terri was dead and Jen was gone too.

"Hey, calm down, everything's fine. It's a fourteen-hour flight from Manila. And then the drive from London took almost four hours. Don't worry, I'm here now."

"Here?"

"At the house."

A sudden chill ran through Mike's blood. He tried to stay calm and say his next words very slowly and clearly because he was certain he was misunderstanding something in this conversation. "Where are you exactly? What house?"

Mike chuckled. "*The* house. You're the one who called me and told me to come here, remember?" His voice became concerned. "Are you okay, Mike?"

"What do you mean? When did I call you?"

"A week ago. July 25th. I've travelled halfway around the world to see you. After you called me, I couldn't get that one thought out of my head: *I have to go see Mike at the house.* Now I'm here and you're not answering the door. Not cool, man."

There was a slight pause and then Rob said, "Oh wait, I see Terri in the upstairs window. She's waving to me. Hi, Terri."

"Rob, no, don't go in the house!"

Rob laughed. "See you in a minute, man. I assume that's you who just opened the front door. You really need to get a brighter light bulb in the hallway. I can't see anything in there but darkness and shadows."

The line went dead.

Mike jabbed at the phone to call Rob back but there was no answer. He tried again. Still no answer. "No," he muttered, leaning back against the oak tree and sinking to the wet grass. "No, not again."

"Dad?' Chris asked, crouching down beside him, a terrified look on his face. "What happened?"

"It hasn't ended," Mike muttered, partly to himself and partly to his son. "It hasn't ended."

The heavy rain hissed down over the grass and gravestones.

AFTERWORD

Hi. I hope you enjoyed *The Haunting of Crow House*. If you could leave a review and let other readers know what you thought of the book, that would be amazing!

And don't forget to look out for more books from me in the future:

Haunted Houses? Check

Monsters? Check

Paranormal Investigators? Check

I hope to see you again soon!

Printed in Great Britain
by Amazon